"It's kinda funny...

little Ashley mused. "You were a dad that didn't, an' now you don't have a family anymore, an' we're a family that used to have a dad but doesn't anymore."

"That is kind of funny," Yance agreed.

"Is that why you been comin' over? Pretendin' like we're your family? 'Cuz me 'n April 'n Billy 'n Nic like it."

Yance had to ask. "And how 'bout your mom? Think she likes it?"

"She's been a lot happier since you been comin' over. She dresses up more, 'n even curls her hair. Think you'll ever take her out with you like she used to go with my dad?"

Yance felt a rush of pleasure that Della might be sprucing up for him. "Think she'd go?" he couldn't help asking.

Ashley shrugged. "Maybe she would. If you asked her."

Out of the mouths of babes. Maybe he would ask her....

Dear Reader,

What would July be without fun in the sun, dazzling fireworks displays—or heartwarming love stories from the Special Edition line? Romance seems even more irresistible in the balmy days of summer, and our six books for this month are sure to provide hours of reading pleasure.

This July, Myrna Temte continues her HEARTS OF WYOMING series with an engaging story about best friends turned lovers. THAT SPECIAL WOMAN! Alexandra McBride Talbot is determined not to get involved with her handsome next-door neighbor, but he goes to extraordinary lengths to win this single mom's stubborn heart in *Urban Cowboy*.

Sometimes true love knows no rhyme or reason. Take for instance the headstrong heroine in *Hannah and the Hellion* by Christine Flynn. Everyone warned this sweetheart away from the resident outcast, but she refused to abandon the rogue of her dreams. Or check out the romance-minded rancher who's driven to claim the heart of his childhood crush in *The Cowboy's Ideal Wife* by bestselling author Victoria Pade—the next installment in her popular A RANCHING FAMILY series. And Martha Hix's transformation story proves how love can give a gruff, emotionally scarred hero a new lease on life in *Terrific Tom*.

Rounding off the month, we've got *The Sheik's Mistress* by Brittany Young—a forbidden-love saga about a soon-to-be betrothed sheik and a feisty American beauty. And pure, platonic friendship turns into something far greater in *Baby Starts the Wedding March* by Amy Frazier.

I hope you enjoy each and every story to come!

Sincerely,

Tara Gavin,
Editorial Manager

Please address questions and book requests to:
Silhouette Reader Service
U.S.: 3010 Walden Ave., P.O. Box 1325, Buffalo, NY 14269
Canadian: P.O. Box 609, Fort Erie, Ont. L2A 5X3

VICTORIA
PADE

THE COWBOY'S IDEAL WIFE

Silhouette®

SPECIAL EDITION®

Published by Silhouette Books
America's Publisher of Contemporary Romance

SILHOUETTE BOOKS

ISBN 0-373-24185-2

THE COWBOY'S IDEAL WIFE

Copyright © 1998 by Victoria Pade

Books by Victoria Pade

Silhouette Special Edition

*A Ranching Family

VICTORIA PADE

is a bestselling author of both historical and contemporary romance fiction, and mother of two energetic daughters, Cori and Erin. Although she enjoys her chosen career as a novelist, she occasionally laments that she has never traveled farther from her Colorado home than Disneyland, instead spending all her spare time plugging away at her computer. She takes breaks from writing by indulging in her favorite hobby—eating chocolate.

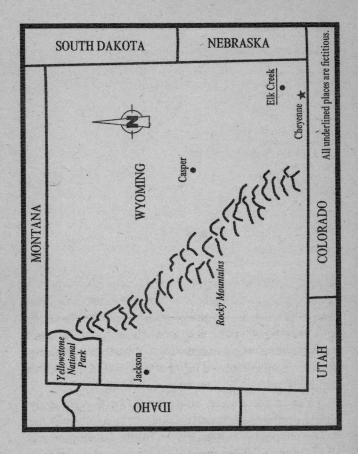

Chapter One

Yance Culhane was in no hurry. It was after four, his day's work was done, he'd just left the feed-and-grain store in Elk Creek, Wyoming—the small town in which he'd been born, raised and spent all of his thirty-eight years—and he was headed home. Rather than rushing, he was more interested in checking out the sky that was thick with gray, low-hanging clouds.

We're in for a long, cold winter, he thought as he turned up the truck's heater.

The temperature outside was below freezing, nearly all the autumn leaves were off the trees and the animals had thicker coats than usual—a sign to any rancher that a hard winter was ahead. But he and his brothers were ready for it. Clint, Cully and he had been running the family spread since their parents had turned it over to them and taken off for warmer climates more than fifteen years ago. But Yance wasn't altogether happy with the prospect of another tough season ahead.

Ordinarily he looked forward to the cold months. He liked the snow. Liked being snug and warm in the house he'd shared with both of his brothers—until recently.

Now Clint was married to Savannah Heller, and they were living in her old house, remodeling it to update it and make it bigger for the baby that was due before long.

Cully and his wife, Savannah's sister Ivey, were living at the Culhanes' main house with Cully's two young daughters, Amy and Randa, and altogether they were a complete family. A complete family that didn't need an uncle hanging around. Yance felt like a fifth wheel.

So rather than looking ahead to spending a cold winter watching ball games or playing a couple of hands of poker with his brothers, or entertaining his nieces, Yance would be on his own; everybody seemed well taken care of and entertained without him.

Yance couldn't help suffering a twinge of jealousy.

He hated feeling sorry for himself. Hated it with a passion.

But there it was. He felt sorry for himself. Sorry for all he'd lost and wished he could have back. And damn if those gray clouds didn't seem like they were hanging around his head.

He tried to shake off the doldrums by reminding himself that he'd have plenty to keep him busy in the next six months. He was doing some remodeling work on what had been the original Culhane house next door to the newer one his father had built thirty years ago. The older home had been vacant for most of that time, so it almost needed to be rebuilt rather than remodeled. Then, when the place was finished—probably early in the spring—he'd move and leave the current house to Cully, Ivey and the girls. But in the meantime it wasn't as if he didn't have one hell of a project on his hands to occupy him.

It was just that it was always so blasted quiet over there....

Yance turned off onto the driveway that led up to both houses. But he looked beyond the white rail fence that lined the way, staring instead at the bright, warm glow of light coming through the windows of the newer house and then comparing it to the cold darkness of the older one that would be his.

Oh, yeah, he was having a pity party for himself, all right.

"Knock it off," he ordered, disgusted.

He drove past both houses to the big barn behind them and backed the truck all the way through the great door that had been left open for his return. Once he was well ensconced in the center aisle of the barn— the feed passage—he turned off the engine and got out, pulling on his heavy leather gloves and shrugging off the thoughts and feelings he'd been having on the way home. He just wasn't going to indulge them.

He rounded the truck and unlatched the tailgate, letting it lie flat so he could reach in to haul out one of the dozen sacks of pig chow that he'd loaded up in town.

That was when he saw that the pig chow wasn't the only thing in the rear of his truck.

"What the...?"

Yance took a closer look to convince himself his eyes weren't playing tricks on him, that he really was seeing what he thought he was seeing.

A boy.

Huddled among the burlap bags of feed was a small boy.

"Come out of there, son," he said. He didn't have a clear enough view to tell who the boy was. Especially not when the child's face was covered down to his brows by a stocking cap and from the chin up to just below his eyes with the collar of his coat, which warmed the air he'd been breathing out in the open truck bed.

"I'm not your son," the boy said with a full measure of contrariness to go with the dark, under-the-brow scowl he leveled at Yance. "I don't got no dad. He died."

Between that statement and finally being able to see the boy's face, light dawned for Yance.

"Billy Dennehy," he muttered more to himself than to the child. "That's you, isn't it, Billy? Come on out of there," he said in a softer tone. "What're you doin' stowin' away in my truck anyhow?"

The boy reluctantly uncurled from among the feed sacks and walked to the end of the truck bed looking as fierce as a six-year-old could.

But fierce or not, when Yance got a closer look at him, what struck him was the fact that the boy was obviously colder than he should be. His cheeks and nose were so chilled they were nearly purple, and Yance could hear his teeth chattering two feet away. Regardless of what had prompted him to hide out in the back of the truck, Yance knew after just that one glance that the boy's temperature had to be what he addressed first.

"Let's go get you warmed up," he said without pre-amble, grabbing Billy under the arms to lift him down.

Once the small feet were on the ground, Yance kept a hand on the boy's shoulder to keep him from trying to run as he guided him toward the main house's back door.

Despite so many lights being on downstairs, no one seemed to be around when Yance ushered Billy inside. But the big country kitchen they stepped into, with its birch cupboards, white tile floor and marble counter-tops, was plenty warm enough, and that was all Yance was interested in at the moment.

"How're your fingers and toes?" he asked as he closed the door behind them.

"Cold," Billy said as if any idiot should know that.

"But are they hurtin' any? Or are they numb?"

"Just cold."

"Let me see you wiggle your fingers."

Billy held out his hands and obliged. When Yance was satisfied that the boy wasn't frostbitten, he said, "Okay. I want you to leave on your coat and hat until you aren't feelin' cold at all anymore. And how 'bout some hot chocolate to help warm you up from the in-side, too?"

Billy scowled and shrugged. It seemed to be as near to an affirmation as Yance was going to get, so he pointed to the stools at the breakfast bar and told the boy to climb onto one of them while he microwaved a cup of cocoa with marshmallows already in the mix— an overly sweet concoction that his nieces were fond of.

"So what were you doin' in my truck?" he asked as he set the mug in front of Billy.

"I'm goin' to Cheyenne to be a bronc buster and never go home again. Did I get there?"

"Sorry," Yance said as if he really was. "We're only about ten minutes out of Elk Creek, at my ranch, which is a pretty far piece from Cheyenne."

"Oh."

"You know who I am?"

"I think you're Yance Culhane," Billy said. "You're one of my dad's friends. But my dad died," he repeated.

"I know that. And it's a sad and sorry thing," Yance allowed.

"If we aren't in Cheyenne now, could you take me there to be a bronc buster?"

"I don't think so. Not without your mom givin' us the go-ahead first."

"She won't."

"Probably some good reasons why not."

"'Cause she's mean, and she don't know nothin' 'bout nothin', that's why."

"Hmm. She's hard on you, is she?"

"If my dad was here, he'd take me."

"To Cheyenne to be a bronc buster instead of makin' you stay home and go to school? Think so?"

Yance asked conversationally and without any condescension to his tone.

But Billy just scowled at him anyway and took a sip of his hot chocolate.

"Feelin' warmer?"

Another shrug and Billy's pulling off his stocking cap were his only answers.

"You know I'm gonna have to call your mom, let her know where you are, that you're all right."

"Call my granddad instead. He'll come and get me."

"Your granddad in Arizona? Where you and your mom and your brother and sisters have been livin' for the last year?"

Billy nodded vigorously.

"Arizona is even farther away than Cheyenne. I don't think it would do any good to call your granddad to come and get you. We're just gonna have to call your mom," Yance said with authority.

He crossed to the wall phone, keeping an eye on the little boy the whole time in case he opted for running, altering his gaze only long enough to dial. He didn't have to look up the number for the Dennehy residence. He still knew it by heart even though he hadn't used it in the year since Bucky's death from a sudden heart attack. But before that he'd called Bucky often enough to have memorized it. Like most of the thirty-something male contingent in Elk Creek, they had been friends. Good friends.

The phone only rang twice before a little girl answered. Since Yance couldn't tell whether it was April or Ashley, Bucky's daughters, he merely asked for her mom.

"She's not here right now—oops, I'm not supposed to say that. I'm supposed to say she can't come to the phone and ask if I could take a message. *Could* I take a message?"

"This is pretty important, and I need to talk to her. Can you tell me where she is?"

"Looking for my brother."

"Your brother Billy?" Yance asked. Her other brother, and the last of the Dennehy children, was five-year-old Nic.

"Yes, my brother Billy." Suspicion crept into her tone.

"Well, this is Yance Culhane. Remember me?"

"Yes." Still suspicious.

"Your brother Billy is with me. So if you could tell me how to get hold of your mom—"

"I'll let you talk to my aunt Kansas," the little girl said in a hurry.

Yance could hear her relaying who he was and what he'd said, and then Kansas Heller got on the phone.

"Yance?"

"Hi, Kansas."

"April says you found Billy." The level of breathlessness mingled with relief let him know just how worried the family was.

"He was nestled in with some pig chow in the back of my pickup when I got home from the feed store. He was hopin' to get to Cheyenne. Something about bustin' broncos."

"Like Linc, I guess," she said, referring to her husband, who'd made his living riding rodeos until marrying Kansas and opening the local honky-tonk saloon. "Della is in town looking for Billy. She took him and Nic in for new shoes, looked away for a minute and Billy was gone. She's just about panicked. Can I track her down and have her come out to your place to get him?"

"Sure. Or I can bring him home myself. Save her the trip."

"Oh, that'd be great. You'll probably have him home safe and sound by the time I find her. It would be a big relief—a *huge* relief—for her to be able to come home and have him here already."

"No problem. He's drinkin' some hot cocoa now, and as soon as he finishes I'll drive him into town."

"Thanks. Thanks so much," Kansas said, following with a quick goodbye before she hung up.

"I don't wanna go home," Billy informed him as soon as the receiver was on the hook. "Moms don't understand nothin' like dads do."

"I'll bet if you worked at it, she could learn, though," Yance said, man to man.

Once more Billy agreed only by not disagreeing. Then, after a moment of what appeared to be sizing Yance up, he said, "Could you talk to her and tell her I'm not a baby no more and I can't wear baby shoes?"

Yance pretended to think it over. "I could probably point that out to her, if you think it might help."

"Good," the boy said victoriously.

And that small victory seemed to be all he needed to convince him to return home because he swallowed back the last of his hot cocoa as if it were a fortifying shot of straight whiskey and hopped down from the bar stool, ready to go.

Yance smiled at him, ruffled up his already unruly hair and said, "Let's see what we can do."

Parked in front of the children's shoe store on Center Street, which was Elk Creek's main thoroughfare, Della Dennehy made quick work of strapping her youngest son into his seat. Then she nearly ran around the car to the driver's side. A simple shopping trip had turned into a frantic search for her other son until the sheriff had tracked her down to tell her that her sister Kansas had called. Billy had been discovered hiding in the back of Yance Culhane's pickup truck, and Yance would bring him home.

That was good news. Great news. But she was still upset. And furious. And doubting her own judgment.

She'd been furious at Billy for throwing a temper tantrum in the shoe store because she wouldn't buy him another pair of cowboy boots when he needed tennis shoes for school. Now she was furious with him for disappearing and putting her through four hours of agony during which she hadn't known where he was, if someone had snatched him or if he'd just taken it upon himself to leave in a snit.

And she was doubting her own judgment because that behavior was due, in large part, to how spoiled she'd allowed all the kids to be in the past year since her husband's death. A year she'd spent with her folks in Phoenix, where sympathetic grandparents had indulged everyone's every whim.

She'd thought that staying away from home, from

all the memories of Bucky, would help her and her four kids cope. And in some respects it had. But the grieving process had its own timetable no matter where the grievers were—there was no escaping it—and in other respects the year away had only caused complications. Like Billy's fit of temper and his running off when she wouldn't give in to his demands the way his grandparents would have.

But whether or not the decision to spend the last year away from Elk Creek had been wise or not, now that they were home again and the kids were in the school where they belonged, Della was determined to get back to life as usual.

Or at least to what would become life as usual on her own with four kids.

Not an easy thing, she thought as she pulled into her driveway.

But thinking about it only made it seem more daunting, so she tried not to. She'd learned in the past year to just concentrate on one thing at a time. On one day at a time. On the moment.

Which meant dealing with Billy when he got there. And trying not to let her anger get the best of her when she just wanted to shake him silly for doing something so foolish.

She stopped the engine and got out of the car, going around to release Nic's seat belt. "Can you carry your new shoes?" she asked, forcing a calmness she didn't feel into her voice.

Nic nodded his head and took the shopping bag into the house.

Della was just grateful that he went without one of the arguments all the kids were prone to these days.

Then she turned her attention to unloading the car.

Bags and packages were piled across the entire back seat, spilling over onto the floor, with even more of them crammed into the trunk. She opened the rear door and left it gaping while she unlocked the trunk lid and then put her keys in the purse she had slung over her shoulder to free her hands. After grabbing as many sacks and packages as she could manage, she headed in the direction of the big Victorian house where she'd grown up.

She loved the old house she and Bucky had bought from her parents when they'd decided to retire to Arizona. It was two full stories of red brick with dormer windows poking out of the steeply sloped roof that left the attic a usable third floor. A double-wide covered porch wrapped the whole lower level, lined at the outer edge with a white rail and thick posts. And on both sides of the oversize front door there were cantilevers that rolled around the corners of the place like huge, turned-out pockets that made for interesting alcoves and larger rooms inside.

The house also had numerous windows. Old-fashioned windows with tiled sills and crisply painted white sashes that should probably be replaced for energy efficiency. But they looked so homey and inviting that Della had never had the heart to update them.

Three tall chimneys stood proudly above the roof, and huge oak trees dotted the expansive yard that stretched ten feet to the east and west before the neighbors' property began, twenty-five feet in back and twenty in front to the sidewalk, then another two feet on the other side of the sidewalk to the curb.

It was a great old house on a great piece of property.

Yet as much as Della loved the place, since returning from Phoenix she hadn't once approached it without the same sinking feeling she felt at that moment.

How was she ever going to be able to handle it on her own?

Bucky had taken care of the yard. He'd cleaned the chimneys. He'd climbed the ladder to wash those dormer windows and clear the gutters of the leaves that fell from all those trees. He'd done most every repair the old place needed—and it always needed something—while Della had done the everyday upkeep.

But now the lot of it was on her shoulders. And every time she looked at it, she felt dwarfed by the prospect.

Aw, it'll be okay, Del....

It was Bucky's voice she heard in her head and it made her laugh wryly to herself. Whenever she felt like this, she imagined she could hear him saying what he'd always said when she'd fretted over something. And even though he wasn't around to help shoulder the load, remembering his simple words helped a little.

With her arms laden with packages, she climbed the five steps that led onto the porch just as Nic slipped through the front door with its wide oval of leaded glass. But before she could follow him, she heard a truck pull up. She turned to see who it was.

Yance Culhane. And only when she actually set eyes on her son, slumped in the seat, his brow beetled into a frown, did she breathe a true sigh of relief.

Then anger set in again, and in an effort to get some control over that, she focused instead on Yance as he parked his pickup behind her car in the driveway.

She'd known Yance all her life. Yance and his two brothers, Cully and Clint. Tall, hard-muscled, good-looking sons-of-guns every one of them. And that hadn't changed in the year Della had been away. If anything, another year's worth of maturity had only made Yance more handsome. And she'd always thought he was the most handsome of the lot.

Not that noticing that meant anything. He was so drop-dead gorgeous it was hard *not* to notice, was all.

He turned off the engine and used the knuckle of one index finger to scratch the bridge of a nose that, even though she couldn't see well at that distance, she knew to be a bit long, very straight and thin and as perfect as it was possible for a nose to be. The barest hint of five-o'clock shadow shaded his sharp jaw and outlined a sensual mouth that had been known to make women go dreamy eyed. A mouth that, it was said, could bestow the best kiss in the whole county. Maybe the whole state. In fact, rumors of Yance Culhane's kisses in high school had started the saying that had trailed all three brothers through graduation—that a girl hadn't been kissed until she'd been kissed by a Culhane.

As Della watched, Yance glanced over at Billy and winked at him with one of those infamous Culhane eyes, which were the second thing that made the brothers stand out from the crowd. Della didn't have to be close enough to see them to know what color they were. Many a slumber party from years and years ago had covered the subject of the differences in the Culhane brothers' eyes in detail. Cully's were crystal blue, so pale they were almost no color at all. Clint's were glacial blue—not an indication of the man himself by any means—but still the shade of ice on a cloudless winter's morning.

But Yance's eyes had more hue to them than either of his brothers'. They blazed like a hot summer's sky....

He got out of the truck then. He had on cowboy boots not unlike what Billy had wanted, blue jeans and a jean jacket that was buttoned halfway up the front. His head was bare of the hat she could tell he'd had on earlier by the ring it had left in his mink brown hair. Hair that was cut short all over and stuck up just slightly on top in a way that might have made another man look messy. But it seemed to suit Yance, leaving him with an appealingly careless appearance that said if he was aware of how attractive he was, he didn't take it seriously.

He went around to the passenger's side of the truck much the way she had rounded her own car moments before. But he walked with a natural, unconscious swagger that was as sexy as Della had ever seen.

And *that* was not something she was accustomed to noticing.

So why had she? she asked herself, surprised by it.

And why was she so aware of the fit of his clothes? Of the fact that hard, bulky thighs filled out the legs of those jeans that hugged narrow hips and a derriere good enough to sell underwear in magazine ads? Of the way his biceps stretched the sleeves of his jacket to their limit? Of the mile-wide span of his shoulders?

Maybe it was only because she'd been away, she told herself. A lot of things around town had looked new to her since she'd been back, had caught her eye in a way they hadn't before. Sometimes it was as if she were looking from a different perspective at things she'd been seeing her whole life.

Sure. This was probably just part of that.

He lifted her recalcitrant son to the ground then pointed the way for Billy to go up the driveway ahead of him.

As Yance followed her son, he glanced in the direction of the porch and spotted her for what seemed to be the first time. Spotted her and did the double take she was getting used to.

It wasn't as if she'd tried to change her appearance— that was certainly the last thing on her mind during the past year. But her appetite had all but disappeared, and so had the thirty extra pounds she'd been carrying—an accumulation of weight left over after each pregnancy.

She'd also let her hair grow, only because she hadn't cared enough to have it trimmed into the close-cropped, matronly style she'd started wearing as a mother of four, too busy to spend much time on herself.

So when people she'd known forever had to take second looks before realizing who she was, she hadn't been surprised. A little flattered, maybe. Especially when they remarked on the improvement.

And now, watching Yance Culhane's brows arch, his eyes widen and his jaw drop slightly, she felt more than a little flattered.

And then a little disappointed when, as Billy and Yance neared her car, Yance's gaze shifted to the open trunk lid and door and all the bags still waiting to be carried inside.

Strange. Very strange, she told herself, unable to fathom why these thoughts and feelings were going through her or why she was having this reaction to a man she'd known forever.

"Hold up, Billy," he said to her son, pausing to take out some small parcels to hand to the boy who was about as eager to help as he was to have tennis shoes instead of cowboy boots.

But Yance didn't brook any refusals, not sending Billy on his way until the boy had all he could carry.

Then Yance hoisted another sack while he maneuvered several others into the grip of large, powerful hands before he resumed that sexy, slightly bowlegged walk toward the house.

"That you, Della?" he asked with a smile that seemed to mingle appreciation with his shock at her new appearance and erase any disappointment she'd felt at the brief lapse in his attention.

"It's me," she confirmed, wondering at the lilt in her voice that sounded almost girlish when it should have had stern undertones aimed at her son.

As Yance climbed the porch steps behind Billy, he nodded over his shoulder in the direction of her car. "Your cupboards bare, were they?" he joked, referring to the trunk and back seat filled with grocery sacks.

Della could feel her face heat up with a blush of embarrassment over what she recognized as more paranoia than anything. "I know it's silly, but there's talk of a blizzard headed our way. Always before when we were snowed in, I could count on Bucky getting out if we needed something. Now...well, I wanted to be prepared.''

"Looks like you're that, all right. You may not have to go those long ten blocks into town the whole winter.''

He was teasing her, but it was gentle enough not to chafe. Instead Della found herself actually laughing lightly. And feeling somehow better suddenly, too. About Billy's antics. About her paranoia. About herself.

But feeling better about Billy's running away didn't mean she could let it go, so she forced one of her most severe mother-frowns onto her face and directed it at her son. "Go up to your room, close the door and stay there until I come to deal with you," she ordered.

Billy scowled, opened his mouth, no doubt to talk back, then glanced at Yance and seemed to think better of it. "Okay," he agreed. Barely.

He took two steps nearer the door, but a clearing of Yance's throat stopped him again.

"I'm sorry I ran away and scared you."

"I'm sorry you did, too. But I accept your apology."

"Do I still haf'ta get punished?"

"Yes, you do."

"I said I was sorry," Billy pleaded, winding up for an argument.

But another clearing of Yance's throat nipped it in the bud. "Okay, okay," the little boy muttered. Then, under his breath he said, "I did wrong and I'll take it like a man."

He still sulked his way into the house like an angry child, but it was an improvement over what Della knew she would have faced without what appeared to be some intervention on Yance's part. She was as grateful for that as she was for his bringing Billy home.

Once her son was out of sight, Della faced Yance again. He was standing only a few feet away and she was suddenly struck by what a big man he was. Something she'd known, of course, but never thought about. Now, however, it seemed impossible *not* to consider it. With six feet three inches of lean muscle towering over her nearly five-foot-four body, it was no wonder his disapproval had made an impression on Billy.

It was a wonder to her, though, why she felt such an impact from the pure potency of the masculinity that went with his stature.

Hoping to shake that response, too, she angled her gaze at the front door rather than at Yance directly. ''Let's get in out of this cold.''

She opened the screen, but he was close enough on her heels to manage to slip an elbow between her and the frame to hold it open for her.

For some reason Della didn't understand, she again felt a blush heat her cheeks. There just seemed to be something about the nearness of him that was having a physical effect on her.

''Thanks so much for bringing Billy home,'' she said then to escape the wild things going on inside her.

''No problem. He was headed to Cheyenne to bust broncos, but the rear end of my truck was as far as he got.''

And that was as much as either of them said before

both Ashley and April came running and talking as fast as short legs and small mouths could go, pinning Della and Yance in the entryway.

"The toilet's makin' that runnin' noise again for a really, really long time, and where the water comes out in the sink is drippin'," Ashley, who was almost nine, announced. Her big, nearly black eyes were wide with the excitement of delivering the news.

"And Aunt Kansas says we better do somethin' about the back door 'cause she couldn't even get it open to let the dog out. We had to take him in the front yard to do his business," a pigtailed, seven-year-old April added.

"And it's cold in here. We had to put on sweaters even though Aunt Kansas turned up the heat 'cause there's hardly nothin' comin' out of our heat thingy in our room."

Della closed her eyes and sighed in frustration. "Where's Kansas?"

"She's in the basement washin' the dog."

"And—"

"I don't want to hear any more right now. Please," she said when April started to add another concern to the pile they were loading on their mother's shoulders. "Just go upstairs and make sure Nic got out of his coat."

"Why don't you see to whatever's goin' on around here, and I'll unload the rest of your car," Yance suggested.

"Thanks," was all Della could say, too overwhelmed to refuse his offer.

It took her a full ten minutes of jiggling the handle

to get the toilet to stop running, and this time nothing she did would keep the sink faucet from dripping. After the sixth attempt she finally gave up and went back downstairs.

Yance had her car unloaded by then, and Kansas was putting groceries away in the kitchen, which was where Della found them both. Along with Barley, the still damp, yellow Labrador retriever that greeted her with eighty pounds of puppy enthusiasm and a foot-long tail that knocked two cans of soup off the pantry shelf.

The animal had been another indulgence of her folks—one they hadn't okayed with her first—and only added to the list of things she was having trouble handling. As was evidenced by the fact that when she didn't pay as much attention to Barley as he wanted her to, he jumped up on her with such force she lost her balance and would have fallen flat on her keister if Yance hadn't reached out and caught her with one of those strong hands clasped around her arm.

And in keeping with the oddities of the past half hour, Della couldn't figure out why she was so ultra-sensitive to the feel of an old friend's helping hand.

"Thanks," she muttered once she was stable again, sounding somewhat shamefaced as she tamped down on still more of those things wreaking havoc with her insides as if she were a marionette whose strings were being pulled by some anonymous puppet master.

"Things under control upstairs?" Kansas asked, helping to yank Della out of the momentary reverie that touch had induced.

"Nothing's under control," Della said in exasperation. Including her and whatever was going on with this heightened-awareness phenomenon. But as if she needed to hide it, she went on to outline what was happening with the plumbing, asking about the door and the gate and thanking Kansas for bathing the dog— no easy feat.

"Sounds like things aren't going real well around the Dennehy house," Yance put in when she was finished.

"The place seems to be punishing me for leaving it vacant for a year. Everything is falling apart. The kids are out of hand, the house needs work and here I am in the middle of it all being a worrywart over a snowstorm," she said with a self-deprecating laugh.

"Hard to get back on track," Yance said kindly.

Della knew he understood only too well.

"What do you say I come over tomorrow to fix whatever needs fixin' around here?" he suggested then.

"Oh, I couldn't impose on you, Yance. It's bad enough that we've dragged you into this mess this afternoon."

"You didn't drag me into anything, and I'd really like to come back, help out."

"And waste your Sunday?"

"Wouldn't be a waste."

Kansas nudged Della's shoulder with one of her own. "Don't look a gift horse in the mouth. Take him up on it."

"I couldn't—"

"Sure, you could," Yance said. "In fact, I won't let you say no. This is something I want to do."

Apparently so because there was a tone in his deep baritone voice that didn't allow for a refusal.

"I could use some help," Della eventually agreed.

"Great. Tomorrow, then," Yance said forcefully. "Unless there's anything that can't wait…?"

"No, everything can. But you really don't have to—"

"I *want* to," he insisted. "What time is good for you?"

They hashed through that with more of Della's trying not to impose, to make it at Yance's convenience, until they finally got it settled.

Then he said, "I'd better take off now and let you get your winter supplies put away."

Della didn't blush at the second round of gentle teasing but instead cracked a joke that made the three of them laugh before Yance denied her offer to walk him out, leaving Della and Kansas alone in the warm red-and-white kitchen.

Kansas waited until they heard the front door open and close again before she said, "I think Yance Culhane had a glimmer of interest in those blue eyes of his every time he looked your way."

That shocked Della as much as what had gone through her mind all the while he'd been there. "You must be seeing things."

"I don't think so. He hardly knew I was in the room. He just kept watching you and watching you…."

"Yance was a friend of Bucky's," Della said as if that meant something.

"So?"

"So he and I have never been more than passing acquaintances."

"So? That was then and this is now."

"Come on," Della said with a shake of her head.

"Come on yourself. Stranger things have happened than that two old acquaintances get together."

"Get together?" Della nearly shouted. "Have you lost your mind? Get together. I'm not ready to *get together* with anybody. And even if I was, what would Yance Culhane, of all people, see in me? I'm a thirty-seven-year-old mother of four, and no one but Bucky Dennehy has so much as taken a second look since I was thirteen."

"Yance was definitely taking second and third and fourth looks."

"You're crazy."

"Maybe I am. Maybe I'm not," Kansas said.

Della just shook her head again and began to empty grocery sacks herself, changing the subject to the weather and if the storm would be as bad as predictions were making it sound.

But in spite of talking about something else, in spite of all her denials about Yance Culhane's having taken an interest in her, there lingered in the back of Della's mind the suggestion that he had seemed a little interested in her. As a woman.

She just couldn't believe it.

She also couldn't believe that it was kind of a nice thought.

Even if it probably wasn't true.

Chapter Two

Yance wanted to get an especially early start to his chores, so he was up before everyone else in the house the next morning. Up and dressed and alone in the kitchen, drinking his coffee, staring out the window over the sink.

From his vantage point, he looked out over the yard, which was a large stretch of lawn beyond a tiled thirty-by-thirty-foot patio that offered the perfect spot for the umbrellaed picnic tables and loungers that took up the space in the summer.

A four-foot-high hedge bordered the lawn, trimmed immaculately and still full of small, brilliant yellow-and-rust-colored leaves that seemed to have swallowed the sun's brightest summer rays to reflect back even now in the dimness of the imminent snow.

The hedge was the dividing line between the backyard and the less-cultivated barnyard beyond it. The barn was the centerpiece of that section of the property. State-of-the-art and twice the size of the house, it was still not large enough to meet all the ranch's needs now that the brothers had built the place up so extensively. But it was a sight to behold nonetheless.

Tall and traditionally shaped, it had gabled walls and a ridged roof with an old rooster weather vane on the highest point. The vane was spinning around in the wind at that moment, making a faint, faraway, quietly comforting creak each time the arrow the rooster was perched on neared the *N.*

Yance had whitewashed the barn to match the house this summer so it was pristine against the black shingles of its roof and the grayness of the cloudy sky. A domed silo stood tall beside it to the right, and to the left was a rail fence surrounding the paddock and separating the pigpens. The springhouse, chicken coops, smokehouse and grain pits weren't far from there, but it was the paddock where Yance's gaze came to rest.

Four horses grazed on the remaining grass. A fifth— a mare—had just been born in May and she was working off some coltish energy prancing as if she were on parade, tossing her head, poking her nose into the breeze.

She was a beauty. Sleek, shiny chestnut brown without another marking on her. Good legs and flanks. Strong shoulders. A mild disposition and a kind of feminine spirit and confidence that reminded Yance of a few women he knew.

Even after he'd finished his coffee, he stood there, taking in the scene. It gave him a deep sense of satisfaction. He was proud of the place he and Clint and Cully worked so hard at building. It was something to be proud of. Successful. Picture-perfect. It was a showplace.

Yet most of the time, he didn't look at it that way. He focused on what needed to be done without noticing much of the finished product. Without noticing just how beautiful it all was.

Funny how a person could look at something day in and day out and not actually see it, not appreciate it. Then, every now and again open his eyes to just how wondrous it truly was.

And for some reason, it occurred to him that not only did the ranch fall into that category, but people did, too. People like Della Dennehy, whose image popped into his mind.

He couldn't believe he hadn't recognized her when he'd first seen her up on her own front porch yesterday. He'd heard talk that she'd come back from Arizona looking like a new woman, but he hadn't given it much heed. Small-town gossip. She'd been away a year, her return was bound to get tongues wagging in one direction or another, and since Della was well-liked and highly thought of around Elk Creek, that talk was more apt to be positive than negative. So of course folks had said she looked so good that they didn't know who she was.

But for once the talk had had some validity to it. She did look like a new woman.

Not that there had been anything wrong with the old Della.

She had always been a fine-looking female. Even with the little extra weight she'd put on over the years.

But now...

Well, now she was better than fine looking. She was beautiful. More beautiful than she'd been even as a young girl.

And she *had* been beautiful as a young girl. Yance remembered it well because he'd had quite a crush on her.

"Ancient history," he muttered to himself. Ancient history that dated back some twenty-five years to the eighth grade when he'd first taken notice of Della Daye.

Unfortunately it had been right about the same time Bucky Dennehy had moved to town and noticed her, too. Noticed her and snatched her up before Yance had had the chance to do or say anything.

And once old Bucky had her, he'd never let her go again. Della had become Bucky's girl. Then Bucky's wife. The mother of Bucky's children.

And Yance's schoolboy crush had gone the way of dust in the wind long ago.

But now Della was Bucky's widow... And damn if he didn't keep thinking about that. About Della as a single woman.

He closed his eyes and studied the image of her in his head. She didn't look a lot like Kansas, but a little. Where Kansas seemed more generically pretty to Yance, Della's features struck him as remarkable. As difficult to ignore. And certainly as impossible to get out of his head since the previous afternoon.

Her nose was thinner and not turned up at the end

the way her sister's was. Her cheekbones were higher and more prominent. Her chin was a tad more pointed and refined. She was just less sweet-and-girlish-looking than Kansas. And where before it had been obvious Della was the older of the two, anyone would be hard-pressed to tell that now.

Yet the improvements all seemed perfectly natural. There was nothing about her that looked like she'd put any effort into this transformation, the way a lot of newly single women did just before they started their manhunt. No, it was as if this new Della were the phoenix rising from the ashes of Bucky's death, as if the experience had reshaped her.

But not without retaining her spunk, her strength, her spirit. Spunk, strength and spirit that still showed in bright green eyes that glittered like firecrackers on the Fourth of July. Spunk, strength and spirit that still showed in the raising of that chin of hers and the toss of her head with its slightly longer hair the same silky, smooth chestnut color as the colt's, now that he thought about it.

Yep, for once it seemed as if the talk around town that Della was a new woman wasn't too far off, and Yance had to admit to himself that she'd caught his eye the same way the pastoral scene beyond his kitchen window had this morning—as if he'd never seen her before.

And now he couldn't stop thinking about her.

Try as he might. And he had been trying. Ever since leaving her place yesterday.

With all its chaos and uproar...

Yance opened his eyes again and chuckled to himself.

He felt bad for what that family was going through, but there was a comical element to it, too. Kids running all over. The house in disrepair. The dog out of control. And Della stocking the larder as if she weren't going to get out again till spring.

It hadn't taken Yance more than five minutes to realize they needed a helping hand. And he was only too willing to give it. In fact, even if his offer to do some work around the house had seemed to come out of the blue, it hadn't. It was something he'd planned to do when Bucky had first died. Yance felt as if he owed his old friend a debt of gratitude that he'd intended to repay through taking up some of the slack in the Dennehy household.

But before Yance had had a chance to approach Della about it a year ago, she'd up and left town.

Since hearing that she was back, he'd been meaning to go over there and offer his services. Only as a handyman or big brother to the kids, he reminded himself when some other, personal services he might offer Della cropped up in his thoughts all on their own.

Maybe Billy stowing away in the back of his truck like that was just a way for the fates to remind him of his good intentions. Spur him into putting them into action.

Not that there was any reason he was dragging his feet or didn't want to help out. Time had just gotten away from him.

He really was happy to take on the task of lending a hand to Della in whatever way she needed now that she didn't have a man around the house. He was happy to finally have a way of making up to Bucky what had been a very big deal to Yance. Happy, too, to have something else to occupy what seemed like too many extra hours in the day lately.

And if he was also happy to have an excuse to see Della again?

That didn't exactly sit well with him.

Even if it was true.

And it was. He was plenty happy at the prospect of seeing her. In fact, he was downright eager.

But not without feeling some discomfort to go with it.

A year might be a fair amount of time for some folks to get back on an even keel. But not for others.

He couldn't tell from the small amount of time he'd spent with Della the day before where Della was in the grieving process, which left him wondering whether or not she was ready yet for a man to be feeling eager to see her.

Or if she'd ever be ready.

Yance wasn't happy with that thought, but he knew he had to face up to it.

New look or no new look, Della might never be ready to move on from Bucky.

Because maybe…just maybe…she would always be Bucky's girl….

"Do I hafta go to school *every* day?"

"Every day during the week. Just like Ashley and April and Billy do," Della explained to her five-year-old as she helped him get ready for church that morning. "But today isn't regular school. Today is Sunday and we're all going to church, then you guys have Sunday school."

"Ick."

"Don't you like Sunday school?"

Nic shrugged. "I like bein' home with you better. We have more fun. At reg'lar school and at Sunday school, too, I hafta do too many stuff. I miss you."

Della gave her youngest a hug. "I miss you, too. But it's only for a little while—especially today. You'll be home for lunch the same as you are during the week."

"But nobody'll be home with you after church like in the rest of the mornings," he said, clearly worried about that.

Nic was the most sensitive of her kids. And since Bucky's death, he'd become ultraconcerned about Della. It was nice but at the same time troubling to her. She worried that the little boy saw her as needing to be taken care of.

"I'm all right the rest of the mornings and I'll be all right this morning, too. You know I have a lot to do."

"But you're by yourself."

"It's okay to be by yourself."

"I think I should stay home with you. Somethin' might happen to you while I'm gone."

Now a little of his own insecurity was showing through, which was something else that had developed in the year that Bucky had been gone. Something all the kids exhibited at one time or another—the worry that fate would snatch her away from them the way it had their father.

"Nothing is going to happen to me," she said gently but firmly. "And you have to go to Sunday school," Della added as she herded them all outside.

She did miss Nic's being home with her in the mornings during the week. The house seemed so big and empty and quiet without him, without the sound of *Sesame Street* as background noise to everything she did. But this morning in particular, she was glad she'd be able to come back for a while without any of the kids. Glad she'd have the place to herself. She didn't want anyone else there for what she had on her agenda.

"Everybody buckle up," she instructed her children once they were all loaded into the car, hearing an unusual note in her own voice. Unusual for the past year, anyway. She sounded upbeat.

She *felt* upbeat, she realized. In fact, she had since she'd awakened this morning. Upbeat and energetic. She was actually looking forward to the day, something she hadn't experienced in what seemed like forever.

But she didn't want to analyze it. Thinking too much about it might spoil it.

She drove the short distance to the white clapboard church with its high steeple, parked in the lot beside it and shepherded her kids in for the Sunday service.

It wasn't any longer than usual, and in another frame of mind, Della would have enjoyed the sermon on being thankful for everyday blessings. But today she was antsy and in a hurry to get back home again.

When the service was finally over, she urged the kids down to the church basement where Sunday school was held in groups separated by age and then rushed back out to the parking lot. She couldn't avoid running into her sister, who was apparently waiting for Linc to drop off Danny with the other kids. Danny was the same age as Nic and had just started both kindergarten and Sunday school, too.

"You're looking bright eyed and bushy tailed this morning," Kansas said.

"Am I?" Della responded as if she wasn't aware of it.

"You must have had a good night's sleep."

"Mmm," was all Della allowed. She actually had had trouble falling asleep the night before. But she didn't want to admit—even to herself, let alone to her sister—that the cause of it had been thoughts of Yance Culhane. And wondering what had gotten into her for that to be the case.

Kansas didn't push it. Instead, she said, "How about coming over to the house for a cup of coffee? You can stay until Sunday school is over and then pick up the kids on your way home."

"No, thanks. Not this morning. I have some things I want to do while the kids are gone," Della said.

"Come on. Dusting and vacuuming can wait."

Della shook her head. "No, really, I have a ton to do." But she didn't offer an explanation of what that ton was. Mainly because it wasn't the housework her sister had suggested it might be, and she didn't want to explain what she had planned.

"Okay," Kansas conceded. "Knowing you, you don't want Yance Culhane coming over to fix things up without having the place spotless."

Della just smiled as if Kansas had hit the nail on the head. Even though she hadn't.

"Don't work too hard," Kansas said by way of goodbye as they separated to go to their respective cars.

"I won't," Della answered.

She got into the driver's side of her sedan and adjusted the rearview mirror, which one of the kids had knocked as they'd gotten out. As she did, she caught sight of her own eyes in the glass.

"You should be ashamed of yourself," she told those green eyes, which looked brighter today than they had in a year.

And she was ashamed of herself—a little anyway. Enough so that she hadn't wanted to admit to her sister what she was about to do.

But not enough to keep her from doing it.

So she hurried home, literally ran inside and locked the door behind her.

Della had never been one to fuss about her appearance. Even as a young girl, "quick and easy, shower and go" had been her style, and girls who paid too much attention to how they looked had seemed vain.

In the year since Bucky's death, that had been all the more true; she'd really not cared what she looked like. So much so that she had barely glanced in a mirror. Makeup, even the small amount she'd worn before, had become something she just didn't bother with at all. And beyond fast swipes of the brush through her hair, she hadn't so much as touched it with a hot roller.

But today—this morning while she was alone in the house for two full hours—she had a goal.

And that was to pay some attention to herself. Starting with a good, long look at what it was that had so many folks gawking, remarking and doing double takes.

She took the stairs two at a time and made a beeline for her room.

It hadn't been easy going back to that room she and Bucky had shared for so many years. Or to the bed. She'd spent a number of nights on the couch downstairs before deciding that maybe buying a new bed would help.

It had. Some. But there had still been a week of crying herself to sleep in it before she'd finally been able to accept that she would forevermore be without him in both the room and the bed.

And now she was uncomfortable doing what she was about to do in that room. Or in the bathroom that adjoined it.

She wasn't exactly sure why. Except maybe that what had prompted this venture was some of those thoughts of Yance Culhane that had kept her awake so late the night before.

But whatever the cause, she gathered everything she needed and went into the hall bathroom that the kids used.

And that was where she threw off the dress and underthings she'd worn to church and stood, for the first time in thirteen months, in front of a full-length mirror to take a good, long, hard look at herself.

What she saw surprised her as much as it had been surprising everyone else. Yance in particular.

Her body was so thin it didn't seem to be her own. Even as a teenager she'd carried a little plumpness. But now there wasn't an extra pound on her anywhere. And neither was there a lot of loose flesh or jiggle to her. She seemed to have shrunk into a firm form that was almost svelte and definitely unlike her earlier self.

Of course, that also meant her chest was much flatter, but as she turned this way and that in the mirror to survey her hips and backside, less buxom seemed like a fair trade for slimmer hips and a derriere that didn't bulge.

And she had a waist, too, she realized. No wonder she was having to tug at her pants all the time to keep them up.

Even her arms and legs looked different. They looked longer. They had shape. Good shape.

It was all very weird to her.

And what about her face?

Sure, her nose was pretty much the same. And her eyes. But the overall shape of her face wasn't. She thought she looked just like her sister Virgie, who had died in a car accident five years ago.

In fact, the longer Della stared at herself, the more she saw her sister's countenance rather than her own.

Not that that was a bad thing. Virgie had been widely known as the prettiest of the Daye sisters.

Always before Della had thought of her own face as doughy looking. Chubby cheeks had played the biggest role in that. But now they were gone. Completely, totally gone. And in their place were slight hollows beneath actual cheekbones. *High* cheekbones.

Oh, yeah, this was very weird.

Even the chin-length bob of her hair worked now when it never would have with those chipmunk cheeks she'd sported before. And she looked younger, too. The way Virgie had when she'd left Elk Creek so many years ago. Younger and somehow more daring. Without a doubt, less like a mother of four.

But it shouldn't matter, she told herself. It wasn't something she should take pride in or something that should please her so much.

Yet it *did* matter. And she was pleased by what she saw.

Along with feeling another rush of guilt.

Guilt for the vanity. For liking the way she looked as a result of grief over Bucky.

For the fact that some of that newfound pleasure in her appearance was because of thoughts of another man. Of Yance Culhane and that jaw-dropping appreciation he seemed to have shown the day before.

"I loved you, Bucky," she said as if she owed her late husband that reminder, as if he could hear it.

She'd loved him with all her heart since she was thirteen years old. And still missed him terribly.

Yet in spite of that, she suddenly had the sense that something inside her was awakening from a deep, deep sleep.

Something that made her feel alive again, allowed her to begin her day in good spirits, eager to take on whatever came her way.

The trouble was, it was all happening in response to the thoughts of Yance Culhane that kept sneaking into her mind. To the fact that she'd be seeing him again today.

And that's what made it all so difficult. That's what made her ashamed of herself.

He was another man. A good-looking, sexy, nice other man she was looking forward to being with.

''It isn't as if he really is interested, or as if anything will happen between us,'' she reasoned to burst the bubble of excitement that rose up inside her every time thoughts of him crossed her mind.

She didn't *want* him to have any interest in her or to have anything happen between them.

Except that there was a secret part of her, deep down, that knew that for the lie it was.

''You've gone crazy, Delaware Daye Dennehy,'' she said to her reflection in the mirror. ''Stark raving mad.''

What other explanation could there be for the gamut of emotions she'd just run through in the past fifteen minutes? In the past fifteen hours? And all over what amounted to nothing but an expression on Yance Culhane's handsome face.

Staring at herself in the mirror she couldn't help thinking that at least if she'd gone crazy she looked good doing it.

And that was what Yance Culhane would see when he got there that afternoon. He wouldn't see her craziness. He'd just see her new body, face and hair.

The new body, face and hair that had made his jaw drop the day before.

And crazy or not, ashamed of herself or not, guilty or not, there was satisfaction in knowing now just what he was seeing…and that it wasn't too far-fetched that he'd liked it.

Della's pleasure in her new appearance didn't last long. Once she'd showered, she was faced with the fact that not having had her hair professionally trimmed had left it scraggly looking no matter what she did with it. And every article of clothing she owned was several sizes too big, which left her with only extremely baggy jeans and an overly large sweater to wear.

She did apply a little mascara and blush, a little lip gloss, so she knew she looked better than she had before, but it was still demoralizing to end up swimming in her clothes and not being able to do anything with her hair even when she tried to.

"You're no fashion plate," she said to herself. "You're still just a plain old hausfrau and mother of four."

But that didn't stop her heart from beating just a little faster, her blood from rushing just a little quicker, when she pulled into her driveway after picking up the kids from Sunday school, getting them a quick lunch from the Dairy King, and found Yance's big white truck parked at the curb with Yance sitting behind the wheel waiting for her.

"What? No packages to bring in today? I thought for sure you'd forgotten something yesterday," he said by way of greeting as they got out of their respective vehicles at the same time and he walked toward her on that sexy swagger of his.

Della waited for him, smiling at his easy, friendly teasing.

"Watch yourself, Culhane, or I might have to hurt you," she joked back, taking in the full view of him as he crossed the yard.

He wasn't dressed much differently than he had been

the day before. He had on jeans and that same denim jacket, which this time was open all the way down but with the collar turned up in a rakish salute that wrapped the back and sides of his thick neck. Inside the jacket he wore a red plaid flannel shirt over a gray henley T-shirt that showed through the gap left by two of the shirt's buttons being unfastened.

He looked clean shaved, not just free of the five-o'clock shadow he'd had the previous afternoon, but *freshly* shaved, as if he'd taken the time to do it before he came. And as he drew up alongside her, Della caught a whiff of a mild aftershave that reminded her of a summer's breeze and seemed to make the wintry day feel less gloomy.

Or maybe it was just Yance's smile at her riposte that brightened her outlook, because it was such a great smile that drew creases down both his cheeks and very appealing lines at the corners of his gorgeous blue eyes.

"How're you doin' today, Delaware?" he asked as they headed for the house together.

She didn't know if she was imagining it or not, but there almost sounded like a note of flirting to his tone. And even if there wasn't, his words had a sweet ring to her ears anyway. For some reason she didn't understand.

"I'm doing fine," she answered. "How are you?"

"Good. Real good."

And for another reason Della didn't understand, it almost sounded as if there was an allusion to that having something to do with her. Or being with her. Or both.

Or maybe she was just imagining that, too.

He raised the big toolbox he was carrying like a suitcase in one hand. "I didn't know what I'd need so I thought I'd better bring everything."

"Probably a wise decision. Even if Bucky has—had—what you need, that doesn't mean I'll know where it is or how to spot it."

They went into the house then. The kids were all peeling off their coats, hats and mittens, leaving them scattered around the entryway floor.

"Hi, guys," Yance greeted them.

A full round of "Hi's" answered him before he enlisted both Billy and Nic as assistants. Nic was clearly included only so as not to hurt his feelings. While Billy wouldn't be much of a help beyond handing Yance a screwdriver or a pair of pliers when he needed them, Nic would likely be no help at all.

Then Yance turned back to Della, and she felt the oddest warmth wash through her at just having those blazing blue eyes aimed at her once again.

"So what's on my agenda besides making the toilet stop running and the faucet stop dripping?" he asked.

"Can you put in a new garbage disposal? I bought it at the hardware store because ours quit two days ago, but I can't get a plumber in from Cheyenne for three weeks."

"Easy. I just put a new one in my place last month."

"And then if it isn't too late or you aren't sick of this stuff, maybe you could take a look at the back door that keeps sticking, and the gate? I just have the gate tied closed so one jump against it and Barley will go right through it."

"No problem." Then, to his two young aids he said,

''How about we start upstairs and work our way down?''

The boys agreed, warming up to the idea as their eyes lit on the toolbox. And with that, the three men climbed the stairs, Nic and Billy leading the way.

Della followed the trio with her eyes, her gaze drawn to Yance's back pockets and the best male rear end she'd ever seen.

Feeling guilty, but enjoying the sight just the same, she carried the memory of it with her into the kitchen, where she decided to put the sudden rise in her energy level into baking a cake.

It only took Yance and the boys about half an hour upstairs before the repairs were accomplished. Then down they came, into the kitchen where Della was just setting the timer for her cake.

''Ready for us in here?'' Yance asked, the sound of his deep voice filling the room with a warmth even greater than what was coming from the heat of the oven.

Or at least that's how it seemed to Della.

And yes, she was ready for him, all right. She'd been counting the minutes until he'd be where she could feast her eyes on him again—much as she had tried not to.

She pointed to the sink. ''It's all yours. The new disposal is in a box inside the cupboard, and I've cleared everything else out from under there.''

''On to phase three, then,'' he said to his small assistants, turning his attention to replacing the disposal.

As he set to the task, Della was more aware of Yance

than she wanted to be. More aware of his every movement as he hunkered down on the floor to peer under her sink, spreading bolelike thighs and bouncing on the heels of cowboy-booted feet. More aware of narrow hips and long, long legs—one of them straight out, the other bent at the knee when he stretched out on his back to work. More aware of big, capable hands as they reached out for the tools he asked for. More aware of the fact that his zipper didn't lie flat...

It wasn't easy, she realized, to have been a happily married, sexually satisfied person for so many years and then to suddenly find herself celibate.

Not that she'd been having sexual thoughts in the year since Bucky's death, because she hadn't. But when she had to tear her gaze away from the bulge beneath Yance's zipper for the third time, it occurred to her that maybe pent-up desires and sexual frustrations were causing this odd reaction to him. Maybe it didn't have anything to do with Yance in particular.

Except that it wasn't happening when she was around any other men....

She forced herself to keep busy doing other things to occupy both her eyes and her thoughts. She made frosting for the cake. She unloaded the dishwasher. She helped April with her homework.

But nothing helped. And when April complained that Della wasn't paying attention, Della could feel her cheeks heat, embarrassed to be caught with her mind wandering to the man lying on her kitchen floor. The man who was setting alight butterflies in her stomach without even trying.

Thank goodness the kids were around as a buffer,

she thought. The trouble was, the blessing of that buffer raised some other feelings inside her that seemed suspiciously like jealousy. Of her own kids, for crying out loud! And their position that close to Yance.

No doubt about it, pent-up desires or not, she'd gone crazy. Maybe they'd *driven* her crazy.

The cake was cool and frosted by the time Yance finished for the day, so Della invited him to have a piece with a cup of coffee.

To Della's secret delight, he said his mouth had been watering over the smell of that cake the whole while he'd been working, and he would love a piece.

With the kids dispatched to other rooms in the house, Della and Yance sat at her big, rectangular kitchen table with its ladder-back chairs to drink coffee and eat cake that Yance complimented profusely.

"Can I pay you for all you did here this afternoon?" she asked when they'd gotten through those compliments.

"No, ma'am," he said forcefully. "This wasn't something I did for money."

"Why did you do it?" she asked, a bit of her usually blunt self showing through.

"Because I wanted to, plain and simple. In fact, I want to do more—if you'll let me."

Why did those butterflies go off in her stomach again? Probably because what it made her think about had nothing to do with dripping faucets or garbage disposals or broken gates.

"There's no more to do. You fixed everything," she said too brightly.

"The leaves need raking, and there are a lot of them

in your gutters—I noticed when I was waitin' for you to get home. And storm windows need to be put on. Billy told me you were frettin' about how to do it yourself and wondered if he remembered from helping Bucky put them on before. But that's not the only things I mean.''

Her heart took wing along with the stomach butterflies.

''What else *do* you mean?''

''I want to help out in general—not just now, but with anything that comes up in the future. And not only with the house. I was thinkin' that I'd like to do some things with the kids. Spend some time with 'em. Be here for 'em. For anything you might need help doing with 'em. I know it isn't easy raising four children without a father, and maybe I could help out on that front, too.''

''Oh, I couldn't ask you to do all that,'' she said in a hurry, surprised by what he was saying.

''You aren't asking. I'm offering.''

''Why?'' she said again with more of that bluntness.

''Because I have a lot of time on my hands with Clint and Cully busy with their own families now. Because it's somethin' I'd feel good about doing and enjoy in the process. Because it's what I want to do for an old friend.''

For Bucky, Della thought. It somehow put a damper on those butterflies and made her feel guilty again for the fact that she'd had such wild flights of fancy in the first place. That she'd had them at all, but especially that she'd had them for a friend of Bucky's. A friend of Bucky's who was only here because of that friendship with her late husband.

"I suppose Bucky would appreciate one of his buddies keeping an eye out for the kids since he can't be here for them," she conceded.

"What about you? You're a friend, too, aren't you?" he asked with a small smile and a lilt to his voice that made it sound once more as if he might be flirting.

But now she *knew* she was just imagining it.

She shrugged. "Well, sure." Except that the thoughts she'd been having about him in the past twenty-four hours were a lot more than friendly.

"Would you hate having me around? Underfoot? Butting in?"

"Would you be underfoot and butting in?"

"I hope not. But maybe that's what you're thinking I'd be."

She was thinking he'd be the source of so many distractions that she really might lose what was left of her sanity. And still the idea of his coming around was too appealing to make anything else matter. Even that guilt that was still hovering over her.

"I think it would be nice to have a little help with things here. And to have a male influence on the kids, too. I debated about coming back to Elk Creek at all because at least in Arizona they had my dad."

"Then you wouldn't mind?"

"Mind? No, I wouldn't mind." Unless she didn't manage to conquer the thoughts and feelings that seemed to be running amok inside her over this man she'd known all her life and never reacted to this way before.

But she *would* conquer them. She swore to herself that she would. She had to.

Yance had finished his cake and coffee. "Guess I'd better head for home," he said as he stood. "Unless you have anything else you need done right now?"

Did he almost sound hopeful that she might say yes?

Della stood, too, and found herself nearer to him than she'd expected to be. Only a few feet in front of him. And she was suddenly struck all over again by what a ruggedly handsome man he was.

So struck that it took her a moment to recall that he'd asked if there was anything else she wanted him to do. "I think you've done enough for one day," she assured him. "I can't thank you enough."

His penetrating blue eyes were on her face in a strangely intense way. On her lips. And she had the oddest thought that she could thank him with a kiss. That maybe he was *thinking* she could thank him with a kiss.

A kiss that would let her judge for herself if the reputation of those subtle, sexy lips was deserved or not.

And more than those butterflies in her stomach or her heart taking wing, what electrified the surface of her skin was an instant, involuntary yearning to do just that. Right there in the kitchen...

"Thanks!" she blurted out in a hurry, snatching herself back from the brink of thoughts, of feelings, of urges she shouldn't be having. That had no place between two old friends. Between her and Yance Culhane. In her kitchen.

"Anytime," he answered.

Della drew her shoulders back and led Yance through the house to the front door out onto the porch.

"I'll be in touch," he told her once they were there.

She knew darned good and well that he meant he'd be in touch as in calling her or stopping by the house. But all on their own, much more provocative ideas of his touching her flitted through her mind.

"But if anything comes up," he added, "just give me a holler."

Della nodded, thinking *way* too much about half a dozen things she could use as excuses to take him up on that and get him back over there.

"Thanks again," she repeated. "For everything." Except the things she was feeling.

Yance said goodbye then and did a hop-skip down the stairs, crossing the span between the porch and his truck on that swaggering walk that she couldn't tear her eyes away from.

And one thing was for sure as she stood there. Nothing that was going through her mind had anything to do with household repairs or kids or being a hausfrau or a mother.

It all had to do with Yance Culhane as a man.

And her as a woman.

Heaven help her.

Chapter Three

The snowstorm that was predicted hit the next morning about half an hour after Della had taken the kids to school. And when it hit, it hit hard. Blizzard force. It dropped four inches of the white, powdery stuff in the first hour alone.

By the end of the second hour, Della's telephone rang, bringing her away from the picture window in the living room where she was watching the snow fall and wondering how bad it was going to get before the kids were dismissed from school.

"Hi, Della. It's Yance," the deep male voice greeted from the other end of the line when she answered the phone in the kitchen.

And that was all it took for her spirits to lift as if they were on the strings of helium-filled balloons.

"Yance," she said, trying to keep her surprise and her pleasure out of her tone.

"You about snowed in over there already?" he asked as if he wasn't close enough for the same storm to have struck him.

"Just about," she said. "Incredible how fast it's coming down, isn't it?"

"Too fast for me to do the fencin' I had planned for today. So how about I come your way, pick up the kids from school and shovel some of this white devil for you?"

Della wasn't helpless. She'd shoveled plenty of snow even when Bucky was alive. And if the roads got too bad to get to the school, she knew a phone call to Kansas at the store would get Linc to pick up her four along with Danny. So she didn't *need* Yance's help.

But *needing* and *wanting* were two different things....

"You don't have to do that," she said, just to be polite when the truth was her heart was racing with delight at the prospect of his coming over today, turning a bleak day suddenly and inexplicably bright.

"I don't *have* to do anything. I want to. Otherwise, I'm gonna end up sittin' here starin' at the walls today."

"I don't believe that for a minute. There's a million things to do on a ranch the size of your place every day, and I know it."

"Naw, we're a finely tuned instrument out here. Everything runs itself," he joked. "So what time does school let out?"

"Nic only goes half day so he's finished at noon.

The rest of the kids go until three, but with weather like this I wouldn't be surprised if they send everybody home at midday.''

"I'll swing by the school at noon, then. If they're havin' the afternoon session, I'll bring Nic home, shovel the walks and go back for the three-o'clock run. How does that sound?''

"Great.'' A huge help. A nice break to a shut-in day. Terrific to see him again…

But she didn't add what was going through her mind. Instead, she said yet again, "But honestly, you don't have to—''

"Better call the school and let 'em know it'll be me pickin' 'em up. I know from experience with my niece Amy how careful they are there about who they allow kids to go home with.''

"Sure. And I'll have them tell the kids what's going on so they'll be looking for you instead of me. If you're sure you want to do this…''

"Positive. No doubt about it.''

Did he really sound as enthusiastic as Della felt?

She thought so. And it set off a little thrill inside her. Even if it meant only that he was a good-natured Good Samaritan. Which was probably the case rather than that his enthusiasm had any more-personal content to it.

"Okay. I guess I'll see you a little after twelve, then,'' she said.

"Count on it.''

They exchanged goodbyes, and Della's first thought the moment the receiver was back on the hook was that the sweat suit she had on would have to go.

She'd already showered, but thinking it was going to be a day of snow shoveling and digging her car out of drifts, she'd just thrown on the old sweat suit, clipped her hair back and forgotten about it. Now she'd have to change clothes and redo her hair.

Well, she didn't *have* to. She could stay just the way she was and face Yance without makeup, wearing a faded sweat suit, with her hair a thatch of unruly raw ends in a lopsided topknot.

In fact, she lectured herself as she stood in the kitchen, still staring at the phone where her hand remained on the receiver, she probably *should* stay just the way she was. After all, what difference did it make if Yance saw her at her most unattractive? It wasn't as if she was trying to attract him.

No, of course it wasn't.

"Here's your chance," she told herself. "Resist the urge. Stop fostering whatever this is that's making you feel and act like some kind of adolescent girl."

But she couldn't do it.

There was no way on earth she was going to meet Yance Culhane at the door looking like she did.

Not that she would want to meet anyone else looking like she did, either, she thought. And that helped soothe her conscience. It made not wanting Yance to see her that way seem more acceptable.

Even if she knew deep down that that was just a rationalization. Even if her hair was neater, even if the sweat suit wasn't old and faded, she'd still go upstairs and change clothes, redo her hair, put on makeup.

Because there was something different all of a sudden about the way she thought of Yance Culhane.

She didn't know why. She didn't know how it had happened. But there it was.

The idea that she was going to spend a little time with him again today put a whole different spin on her outlook just the way knowing she was going to see him the day before had. He'd been creeping into her thoughts almost constantly. His image seemed to have taken up permanent residence in her mind to send little shards of delight raining through her.

And since his departure the afternoon before, she'd been wondering the same thing—what if he really had been leaning toward her when they were putting an end to his visit? What if she hadn't been just imagining it? What if he'd been about to touch her? To kiss her?

She couldn't for a moment believe any of that was actually true.

But that didn't stop her from thinking What if?

Lord, she shouldn't be letting her mind wander like this.

She shouldn't be about to primp for something as innocent as an old acquaintance's coming over to shovel snow off her walks.

She certainly shouldn't be wondering if Yance really had leaned mere inches toward her or thought the same wild things she had.

And she most definitely shouldn't still be holding on to the phone receiver to keep even that remote sense of connection with him....

And yet, knowing all that, telling herself all that, believing all that, still didn't keep her from sliding her hand off the phone in a caress as tender as if it were his broad biceps. Then she made a beeline for her room to shampoo her hair, tear through her closet in search of something that came close to fitting and break out the mascara and blush for the second time in two days.

Because something had gotten into her.

She just didn't know what it was.

Or how to conquer more of that guilt that went along with it.

Snow had never looked so good to Yance.

Not that he ordinarily hated winter. It was just that a blizzard like the one he was driving through at that moment—especially this early in the season, when the trees weren't yet bare and the ranch wasn't fully winterized—could be a real pain in the neck. Broken branches, stranded calves and any number of other unforeseen problems could accompany premature bad weather.

But pain in the neck or not, at the first sign of heavy snow this morning he'd felt like jumping for joy. It had given him a purpose, supplied just the excuse he'd been racking his brain for. The excuse to see Della.

That crush he'd had on her in the eighth grade seemed to be cropping up like a jack-in-the-box when the lid popped open. And she might appear to be a new woman, but this was making him *feel* like a new man. Or like a kid again.

Damn if he hadn't been thinking about her nonstop for nigh onto two full days now. Daydreaming about her without even trying. Staying awake nights wondering what she was doing, if she was asleep, how she looked with that dark chestnut hair spread out against the pillow, with her eyes closed and those long lashes dusting her cheeks. Wondering if she slept on the right side of the bed or the left. Wondering what she wore to bed.

Yep, it was strange, all right. Strange to be mooning over a woman the way he hadn't thought he ever would again. Strange for that woman to be someone right under his nose all this time. Strange for that woman to be Della—the new and improved Della. Strange to be so drawn to her, so attracted to her, that when he was standing in her kitchen the afternoon before, he'd found himself craving to touch her—even just her arm—craving to kiss her, so much that he'd actually been leaning in to do it before he realized it.

It wasn't as if he'd even been *thinking* about kissing her. He hadn't been. He hadn't had any intention of that. Not consciously. It was just as if his body was responding to her all on its own, to the urges that were rising in him, bypassing the thought process completely and surprising the hell out of him.

Maybe *strange* didn't cover what was going on inside him.

And what about Della? he asked himself.

Was it possible for her to see him in any light other than that of a lifelong acquaintance? An old friend of her late husband?

And if she did, what then? Bucky and Della were known as the ideal couple, and Yance himself had believed it. Filling Bucky's shoes would be no easy thing.

And she had four kids to think about.

Four kids *he* should think about.

Four kids.

This was not an uncomplicated situation. Not by any stretch of the imagination.

Yet none of that daunted Yance as he pulled into the school parking lot.

"It should, though," he told himself out loud as if to reinforce the gravity of it all. "You should be thinking seriously about what it is you're doin' here."

But even a firm warning didn't seem to matter. The only thinking he could do was about Della herself. About how much he liked the way she looked. About how much he liked the sound of her voice. About how much he liked how terrific she smelled. About how he even liked her bluntness when she'd come right out and asked him why he was offering his services. And about what liking all that did to him. About how it churned him up inside in a way that no one had since Nancy.

Okay, so it probably wasn't common for two people who had known each other their whole lives to wake up one morning and take sudden notice of each other. But common or uncommon, it wasn't impossible.

At least not for him.

He didn't have the slightest idea if any of this was true for Della.

Still, though, for just a split second in her kitchen the previous afternoon, he'd thought she might be doing a little leaning his way, too. With her chin tilted just a tad. Her lips parted only enough to make them kissable.

Or maybe the craving in him had been so strong that he'd just *thought* she might be feeling some of the same attraction, some of the same stirrings, he was.

And maybe the lid popping open on that jack-in-the-box was just going to make him end up the way he had in eighth grade—hiding a crush on someone whose heart belonged to someone else.

But the someone else was gone now, Yance reminded himself, feeling a twinge of guilt for it.

And as highly as he'd thought of Bucky, as much as he'd considered him one of his best friends, the fact was that no one else was on the playing field.

And he couldn't help thinking that maybe this time that crush he had on Della might actually go somewhere.

If he took things real slow. If he didn't push her. If he could just keep coming up with reasons to see her.

Yep, he felt like a kid again. And not all of that was good, because like a kid he also felt unsettled and nervous about saying and doing the right thing. About not going overboard. About wanting like hell to know if she was as attracted to him as he was to her.

Oh, no, *strange* didn't even begin to cover what was going on with him.

"And if you had any brains you'd be fightin' it all instead of givin' in to it," he said, reminding himself that she could very well not be ready for what he was feeling, that he should give some serious consideration to getting involved with the mother of four kids—if he and Della did get involved.

But he couldn't bring himself to fight anything. Not when the image of Della came into his mind again. Not even when the image of her four kids followed.

Instead, he discovered that the whole family had an appeal for him. Being a part of it...

Then it occurred to him that maybe he should examine his motives and what needs of his own were being filled by being with Della and her kids.

But when the noon bell rang from inside the school, his heart took another of those jumps for joy. He knew that in not more than a few minutes, he'd be leaving the school lot, driving the ten blocks to Della's house and seeing her again.

And no matter how hard he tried, he just couldn't not be as happy as a dog with a bone at that prospect.

Della had been right about the school closing down at noon. So when Yance arrived at her house, it was with all four kids in tow and Della could breathe a sigh of relief to have her family home safe and sound.

Her family and Yance.

He set to work right away on shoveling the sidewalks and the driveway, enlisting the help of her whole brood. He even had Nic working diligently on the porch steps with a small gardening spade.

But as Della stood at the picture window in the living room again, watching, it wasn't Nic or Billy or Ashley or April her attention kept drifting to.

It was Yance.

It should have been illegal for any one man to look as good as he did.

Once again he had on jeans and the worn denim jacket—this time with a turtleneck on underneath it that was as white as the snow. Snow he was lifting in huge shovelfuls as if they weighed nothing at all. Not straining, but merely mastering it with the strength of broad,

broad shoulders and arms so muscled she could see them bulging within the confines of his coat sleeves.

And every time he bent over to scoop up another load, she couldn't keep her eyes off his derriere.

What a rear end!

Anything that terrific should be outlawed.

And so should gawking at it the way she was, she reprimanded herself.

But she still couldn't stop. Not when what she was seeing was such a feast for the eyes. A feast she was filing away in her memory to replay again and again in her mind. Tonight. In her cold bed…

No, she couldn't stop watching Yance. It was as if she were glued to that window as the sight of him wreaked havoc with her senses. It made the surface of her skin tingle, her shoulders straighten and her breasts rise within the bulky sweater she was wearing.

But appreciating a vision as incredible as Yance presented was only normal, she reasoned. Maybe it was even a good sign. After all, didn't the ability to recognize his pure masculine beauty, the hard, honed body he sported, mean she was emerging from some of her grief? And wasn't that healthy?

It seemed like it should be considered healthy by most people.

So how come she still felt as if she were indulging in a guilty pleasure? A *really* guilty pleasure?

Probably because she just couldn't help feeling as if she were being unfaithful to Bucky. Maybe it wasn't rational. Maybe it was unwarranted. But there it was anyway.

But no matter how guilty she felt, it was still a pleasure.

And no matter how hard she tried, she couldn't tear her eyes away from the vision he presented.

When the shoveling was finished and Della expected everyone to come inside, she slipped away from the window so as not to get caught watching Yance. Even though it could easily have been said that she was keeping an eye on her kids, she knew better and went into the kitchen to prepare hot chocolate for everyone.

But rather than the sounds of Yance and the kids descending upon the house, what she heard moments later was the doorbell ring.

Wondering why her kids would ring the doorbell instead of just coming in, she hurried to the entryway. As she neared the door, she could see through the oval of leaded glass in the top half that it was Yance on the other side of it. With her kids behind him like Christmas carolers.

"We want you to come out and play," he said when she had the door open. "This is some goo-ood snowman-makin' snow. And I understand you do a snow angel that's somethin' to see."

"Wouldn't you all rather come in for hot chocolate?"

"Not yet," Billy answered from behind Yance, a mischievous grin on his face.

"Yeah, come on, Mom. Come and do the angel for us," April added with a giggle.

"Why do I feel like I'm being lured into a trap?" Della asked.

"Paranoia?" Yance suggested. "What kind of a trap could there be in building a snowman with us?"

Della glanced from one to another to another and saw the twinkle of mischief alive and well in each of her kids, along with a much too innocent expression on Yance's gorgeous face.

But even so, she couldn't resist. Not with Yance smiling so alluringly and her kids beckoning with the first bit of carefree, childish glee she'd seen in them in a year.

"I'll get my coat and gloves. But I don't want you guys out too much longer. It's about time to get warmed up."

It seemed like forever since she'd done anything just for the fun of it, and anticipation of that caused the excitement that was coursing through her.

Or at least that's what she tried to believe while she hurried into her coat and yanked on her gloves as if the house were afire, trying to convince herself that the excitement didn't have anything to do with being thrilled to have been invited to join in the activities with Yance.

"Okay, you guys, where are you?" she called when she stepped out onto the front porch and found no one in sight.

"We're buildin' the snowman on the side of the house," Yance answered from that direction. "The snow's better over here."

Della heard more giggling and then she really knew something was up. But still she pulled the door closed behind her, went across the porch and down the steps.

And that was when she was bombarded with snowballs from both sides. Yance and Nic were hiding around the corner of the porch, and Billy, Ashley and April were crouching just below the latticed skirt.

"No fair!" Della yelled even as she laughed and shook off the wet clumps that clung to her coat. Then she leaned over as if to brush snow off her pant leg and snatched up a big glob of it from the ground instead to fling up toward the man she knew to be the instigator of this trick—Yance.

The kids all squealed with delight as she caught him off guard, giving him a face dusting of frigid white powder.

"Oh, now you're in for it," he growled playfully.

With all four kids on Della's side once Nic switched allegiance, a rollicking snowball fight ensued until everyone was sopping wet and nearly falling down laughing.

"Truce! Truce!" Della finally shouted even though Yance was taking the worst of it. "We're all going to catch cold if we don't get inside and warm up."

April, Nic and Billy groaned.

"We gotta do angels," Billy reminded.

"Yeah, angels," April and Nic chimed in.

"What do you say, Del? Let me see your stuff," Yance added with just the faintest hint of sensual innuendo in his tone and those blue eyes of his glittering too much for Della to doubt what she'd heard.

"I'll show you my stuff, all right," she countered, letting bravado gloss over his more adult edge as if she hadn't caught it.

Then she purposely fell backward in the snow, proceeding to flap her arms and legs so they smashed down sections that appeared to be an angel's wings and skirt.

It didn't occur to her how ridiculous she looked doing it until she glanced up to find Yance standing above her, grinning from ear to ear while the kids were off making angels of their own.

Della sat up, taking with her another handful of snow and tossing it at him. "Don't laugh at me, Culhane," she warned with a grin of her own.

"Am I laughing?" he said, arching one eyebrow at her.

"Inside you are."

He held out a hand to help her up, and Della took it, not having any idea that that mere meeting of his glove around hers would send little pulses of electrical shock through her.

He pulled hard enough for her not only to get to her feet, but also to end up nearly against the wide expanse of his chest, where she caught a heady whiff of that same aftershave he'd had on the day before.

"You can't even start to know what's going on inside me," he said softly enough for her ears alone and with a whole lot more of that sensual undertone laced into his voice.

Enough to make Della blush even as a delicious warmth that had nothing whatsoever to do with embarrassment flushed through her and made her forget the cold air all around them.

Then, just as quick as that, he let go of her, leaving her wishing much too much that he was right back there, in front of her, holding her hand, smiling down into her face and saying things that he shouldn't be saying.

But instead, as Della stood there in the brilliant flash of that moment's intimate attention, Yance hollered for the kids, telling them it was time to go in.

"Where's Ashley?" he asked then.

That was enough to drag Della out of her reverie. She glanced around, counting heads, and discovered that her oldest daughter was indeed nowhere in sight.

"Ash go'd in a long time ago," Nic offered.

"Is she sick?" Della asked.

"No. You know. She got sad again," Nic said with a shrug.

"Well, let's go in and have hot chocolate. Maybe we can cheer her up with that," Della said. Then, before there could be any doubt she was including Yance, she added, "Although you can have coffee if you'd rather."

"Hot chocolate sounds good to me," he answered as they followed the three wet munchkins inside.

There was a lot of chaos as coats, boots, hats and mittens were all removed, and then April, Billy and Nic joined Ashley in the living room, where she was sitting dejectedly in front of the television watching cartoons.

"Want some hot chocolate, Ash?" Della asked.

"Okay," Ashley answered as if she honestly didn't care one way or another.

Yance didn't need an invitation to follow Della into the kitchen. He just came with her as if it were something he'd always done.

But he waited until they were down the hallway beside the staircase and into the bright kitchen before he said, "Did I do something to upset Ashley?"

Della glanced up to find a frown of concern furrowing his handsome brow, and his worry that he might have caused her daughter's mood went a long way in softening Della's heart.

"No, it isn't you," she assured him in a hurry. "Tomorrow is Ashley's birthday. She'll be nine."

"That's a little young to be frettin' over her age, isn't it?" he asked with a slight laugh that didn't cover up either his confusion or his continuing concern.

Della smiled at him, taking in the powerfully handsome vision of him without his denim jacket on. The white turtleneck hugged his chest, his shoulders and his biceps like a loving second skin and gave her an intense craving to smooth her palm over it all to test the hardness beneath. The craving was so intense that it made her mouth go dry and reaffirmed her earlier thought that it should be illegal to look that good, that masculine, that sexy....

She went to the sink and took a quick drink of water to moisten her mouth before she could answer his question about her daughter's fretting over her age.

"It isn't how old Ashley is that's bothering her. It's the birthday itself. Bucky always treated each one of the kids to a special, one-on-one dinner on their birthdays—just Bucky and the child of the hour. Then he'd bring them home to the party I give for the occasion."

"And Bucky isn't here now to do it," Yance finished for her.

"Last year my dad did the honors to keep up the tradition, and this year I suggested I do it while Kansas does the party preparations for me. But none of the kids thought it was too special to be taken out by Mom, and Ashley declined my offer. So now she's just feeling bad and missing her dad even more.''

Della had heated milk while she talked. Judging it warm enough, she poured it into the six waiting cups.

"How about I do it?" Yance said after a moment of watching her.

"The birthday dinner?"

"Sure. It's worth a try. If she'll go with me, I'll make it as special as I can for her."

A red flag went up in Della's mind just then. It had surprised her how much the kids had warmed to Yance between the previous day's repairs and today's snow play. Yance's taking Ashley for a special birthday dinner might be the solution to her daughter's blues.

But what if Yance's attentions were nothing more than a passing kindness? The sort of kindness people bestowed in the early aftermath of a death but didn't keep up? The kids might not understand that his attentions weren't something to count on. They might be disappointed, hurt. They might suffer another loss.

"I appreciate the offer, but—"

"Don't start with that 'I don't want to impose' business again."

"It's not only that." She explained what her concerns were in as tactful a way as possible.

"This is more than a passing thing, Della," he said as if he had no doubts about it. "I want to make a commitment to these kids. To keeping an eye on 'em. To filling in for Bucky where I can. And I want to do it over the long haul."

"Why would you want to do that?"

Something about her blunt question made him smile down at her so warmly that that flush of heat rippled through her again.

"Let's just say one good turn deserves another."

It finally dawned on Della that Yance's good deeds were due to more than just the friendship he and Bucky had shared.

"This is because of what Bucky did when your wife and son were in that car accident three years back, isn't it?"

"He was the first to happen by," Yance said in confirmation. "Nancy was already dead. The hospital told me the stroke she had was so massive that she died almost instantly and that was when the car spun out of control and rolled on that stretch of road out to our place. But the baby was still alive when Bucky got there. He kept Jeremy that way by givin' him CPR until the hospital helicopter arrived. Jeremy only lived a few hours, but it was still a few more hours I had with him. Maybe that doesn't seem like much, but it was long enough for me to hold my boy once more before he passed." Yance's throat seemed suddenly constricted, and he stalled for a moment.

Then he said, "That meant more to me than I could ever put into words. So I'd like to put it into actions now, with Bucky's kids. For as long as they need me."

Della could see how strong his feelings were. She'd known all along how hard it had been for him losing his wife and son, but she'd never realized that what Bucky had done had had so much impact on him. Bucky had viewed what he'd done as just what anyone would have. He'd always regretted that it had still turned out so badly, but to Della's knowledge, he'd never seen it as anything Yance owed him for.

Clearly that was how Yance saw it, though.

But before Della could say anything, he smiled at her and lightened the tone. "Besides, I'm surrounded by married couples now. All my runnin' buddies are hitched up, and I'm like the thorn among roses. You might as well put this old thorn to some good use."

Della couldn't begin to see Yance as a thorn of any kind.

But still she was leery. "I'm afraid of the kids getting too attached to you." And maybe of herself getting attached to him, too. "I know your intentions are good, but you could meet someone and fall in love, get married and have kids of your own any time. And if that happens, you aren't going to want to keep playing big brother to my four."

Just posing the possibility of a woman in his life, of his falling in love with her, made Della clench up inside.

But not only for any disappointment that might result if her kids were left with unmet expectations. This had to do with her....

"I'll tell you what," he said into her musing about why such a thing should have any effect on her at all. "I won't say boo to those kids without your okay first. You see that my lookin' after 'em here and there is puttin' any one of 'em in line for a disappointment of any kind, and all you have to do is say the word. I'll back off. Or do whatever it takes to not disappoint 'em. And as for my marryin' and havin' a family, well, that isn't on any horizon I can see. And if it should happen,

I give you my most solemn promise that it won't stop me from doin' right by those kids, just the way Bucky did right by mine.''

Lord, but the man was difficult to resist. In every way, including his persuasive powers, since he just seemed to have so much conviction.

''Maybe if we took it a little at a time,'' she finally conceded, hoping she was doing the best thing for her children. But at that moment it seemed as if she'd be doing them a disservice if she didn't allow them Yance's attentions.

''So it would be all right if I invited Ashley to a birthday dinner?''

''I guess you could test the waters with her. But don't feel bad if she turns you down.''

Della picked up three of the mugs of hot chocolate, and Yance took the other three without being asked, following as she headed for the living room.

Once the drinks were distributed—along with warnings to be careful not to spill—Della watched Yance approach her oldest daughter about dinner the next night.

And she had to admit that she was impressed.

As if Yance Culhane hadn't been impressing her all along.

But this time she wasn't only impressed by his looks and his charm, which he used to a mild degree on Ashley. She was also impressed by the great delicacy he used with the little girl and the deep understanding he showed of how much she missed her father as he asked if maybe he could stand in for him.

Ashley was pretty down in the dumps, so it wasn't

an easy sell. But Yance managed to persuade her in a way that left the little girl visibly in better spirits, winning her over.

"You're smooth, Culhane," Della said as she walked him out onto the front porch a short time later, after he'd finished his hot chocolate and confirmed his date with her daughter. But she said it softly, not facetiously, her tone full of the gratitude she felt for how he'd handled this problem.

He tipped an imaginary hat at her. "Just doing my job, ma'am."

Despite their joking around, his eyes sought out hers, holding them in a gaze that gave her the sense that he was enjoying the sight of her and enjoying her company as much as she'd been enjoying both the sight of him and his company all afternoon.

And this time, when she thought he might be leaning toward her, she was right. Leaning toward her enough so he could peck a light kiss on her forehead before he backed up again.

"See you tomorrow about five," he said in a deep, quiet voice as intimate as if the kiss had been passion filled.

And it couldn't have left her more stunned if it had been.

"Tomorrow. Five," she repeated dimly.

He grinned and winked at her with a bit of the devil to it, said goodbye and left her standing there.

What on earth was going on? Della asked herself as she watched him get into his truck and drive off through the snow.

But she didn't have an answer for what was going

on with Yance any more than she had an answer for what was going on with her. Inside her. In response to him.

She only knew that whatever it was, it scared her silly.

Especially when she realized that she was standing in the middle of a blizzard watching him go and wondering what it might have been like if he'd kissed her on the lips rather than on the forehead.

And wishing he had.

Chapter Four

"Did you bring it?"

"How about saying hello to Aunt Kansas first?" Della suggested to her daughter late the next day as Della opened the screen door to let her sister in.

Kansas ignored Della's reprimand and said, "Happy birthday, Ash. Yes, I brought it."

Kansas handed over a small brown paper bag from which Ashley took an especially elaborate barrette for her hair.

Ashley had seen the barrette at the general store—the store Kansas had taken over when their parents had retired. And once Ashley had seen the barrette, she'd wanted it. She'd used the occasion of her birthday—or more specifically, of her birthday dinner with Yance—to ask for it. Not as a gift, however. She'd made it very clear that gifts were only to be toys. Even though she

was beginning to be interested in the way she looked—
to the point of wanting fancy barrettes for her hair—
nine was not so old that she didn't still want toys.

"Okay, Mom. Now, do it like I told you. Like from
the magazine. On the side."

They hadn't moved from the entryway, but Della
knew Ashley couldn't wait to have the barrette put in
her hair. She used the comb Ashley had brought with
her when she'd heard Kansas arrive and swept one side
of her daughter's shoulder-length brown hair up and
back, where she caught it dramatically over the little
girl's right ear.

The style was too mature for a nine-year-old child,
but Della didn't point that out. This was a special evening, and the fact that Ashley was no longer depressed
about it, but was anxious and excited about her birthday now, was not something Della had any intention
of putting a damper on.

Besides, Della couldn't help feeling anxious and excited about Yance herself. And she wasn't even going
out to dinner with him. Unfortunately. She'd be left at
home to set up for Ashley's party, just the way she'd
always done on the kids' birthdays in years gone by.

But this was the first time she'd ever suffered so
much as a twinge of jealousy over it. That same twinge
she'd suffered every other time her kids had Yance's
company and attention and she didn't...

"There you go. Now you're all set," Della said
when she'd finished Ashley's hair. Then both she and
Kansas complimented the little girl profusely.

But Ashley seemed more interested in straining for

a glimpse out the leaded glass in the door to see if the truck they could all hear outside was Yance's.

It was. He was five minutes early. And looking traf-fic-stoppingly handsome in a pair of khaki-colored jeans, a Western-cut brown sport coat over a cream-colored Western shirt and a bolo string tie with a gold clasp that wrapped the braided leather like a coil just below his open collar button.

Ashley giggled at the first sight of him coming up to the house and Della understood that sentiment, too. As she watched his approach over her daughter's head, he made her go giddy inside and want to giggle just the way Ashley had.

But she worked to control it and opened the door to let him in.

Once the greetings were out of the way, he gave Della a conspiratorial wink over Ashley's head and proceeded to reaffirm what Della and Kansas had said about how nice the little girl looked. Then, from behind his back, he produced a tiny corsage of one white rose-bud among a bed of baby's breath.

Ashley couldn't have been more delighted if she were a grown woman accepting a dozen long-stemmed roses. She beamed as Della pinned the flower to her blue jumper.

Yance helped Ashley on with her coat and, once she was buttoned up, he offered his arm and tossed another wink and a general goodbye over one broad shoulder as he led the birthday girl out.

Della watched them all the way to the truck, where he helped her daughter into the passenger's side. But even then, she didn't turn away. Instead, she lingered until Yance rounded the vehicle and got in behind the wheel.

"Hmm, looks like the wrong Dennehy is going on this date," Kansas said from behind her.

"It isn't April's birthday," Della answered, being purposely obtuse.

"I didn't mean April. I meant you," Kansas persisted as they both picked up the sacks of party paraphernalia that Kansas had brought over from the store in addition to the barrette.

"I couldn't go on a date. With anybody," Della said as if it were the last thing on her mind when, actually, she'd been imagining what it would be like if Yance Culhane had been picking her up tonight rather than Ashley.

"Why couldn't you go on a date?" her sister asked as they headed to the kitchen. "You're a single woman now. Maybe not by choice and maybe not happily, but you are single."

"I'd feel too guilty," Della admitted, for the first time saying out loud what had been racking her every moment since she'd realized she was in the throes of a fierce and inexplicable attraction to Yance.

"Guilty? For what?"

Della shrugged. "I feel like I'm being unfaithful to Bucky."

"Wait a minute. First you said you *would* feel guilty, as in if you went on a date some time in the future. Now you say it as if you're *already* feeling guilty for something."

Della grimaced but decided maybe talking about it with Kansas would help. "I am."

Kansas perked up like a dog hearing the approach of a train it was bound to howl at. "Okay, spill it. What's going on that I don't know about?"

"Nothing's going on at all. It's just me."

Della went on to explain the wild things that were happening inside her every time she saw Yance or thought about him.

"So not only is he interested in you, but you're interested in him, too. Great, great, great!"

"No, no, no. Nobody said he was interested in me. And I can't be interested in him."

"Why can't you?"

"I *told* you, Kansas."

"You are not being unfaithful to Bucky."

Della didn't respond to that. It seemed futile to refute it again. No matter how emphatically her sister said it, it didn't change how Della felt.

"Let's think about this," Kansas suggested, seeing she hadn't gotten through to Della. "Is there some cultural or tribal custom you're bound by—like being buried with your husband?"

Della just rolled her eyes at that.

"No, nothing I can think of," Kansas said, answering her own question. "How about some religious tenet?" She pretended to consider it. "Nope, no religious tenet I can think of says that a widow can't go on with her life, meet someone new, fall in love—"

"Yance is not someone new."

"And you're splitting hairs."

"I can't help how I feel."

"Of course you can. Just knock it off. I know you and Bucky had that talk every couple has at one time or another—the 'if something happened to me would you remarry?' talk—because I was there for it at least once that I can recall.''

''Sure, we joked around about it.'' Then more sheepishly Della admitted, ''And we talked about it not so jokingly when Linc came back to town and started seeing you.''

''Let me guess—you had that talk then because you were upset that I was getting involved with the husband Virgie left widowed.''

Della couldn't look Kansas in the eye.

''Come on, spill that, too,'' Kansas urged.

''Okay. It was hard for me to see the husband of one of my sisters going after my other sister—even though Virgie had been dead almost four years. It was weird.''

''And Bucky talked you out of thinking it was weird—that's my bet,'' Kansas said.

''Yes.''

''And now it isn't even something you think about anymore. Linc and I are together. We're a couple. A family. And that's that. Life has gone on.''

''Yes.''

''Because if our lives hadn't gone on, it still wouldn't have brought Virgie back. Not all the grief or suffering, not decades of refusing to move forward or start new relationships or anything else would have brought Virgie back.''

''Granted. But—''

''But nothing.'' Kansas's voice softened. ''We all know how much you loved Bucky. But, Del, he's gone. Nothing will bring him back. And I heard him say to you that if something ever happened to him, he'd want you to marry again.''

"Just not have sex," Della added with a laugh because that's what her late husband had added when they'd joked about this.

"And I don't have any doubt that when the two of you talked about Linc and me, he told you the same thing then, too—that he wouldn't want you to spend the rest of your life alone if something happened to him."

"He said almost exactly that. That we had such a good thing between us, that if either of us ever lost the other, he'd wish we could find what we'd had together again with someone else. The way Linc was finding it with you."

"Sounds like permission to me."

"Permission?" Della queried.

"What else would you call it? Certainly not something for you to avoid or feel guilty about. Bucky wouldn't have wanted you punished the whole rest of your life because he wasn't here to be a part of it. That wasn't like him."

"No, it wasn't. But—"

"But nothing," Kansas said again. "You wouldn't be doing anything wrong to have a relationship with another man. You wouldn't be cheating on Bucky. You wouldn't be defiling his memory. Not a soul in this town would begrudge you going on. And it also wouldn't mean you'd be forgetting Bucky or losing sight of what you had together or doing anything that would diminish how terrific that was. It's just that the sad truth is that it doesn't exist anymore. But if you had a chance for a second round of it—whether it's with Yance Culhane or anyone else who might come along—you not only have Bucky's permission to do it, but you owe it to yourself to do it. Without feeling guilty. Without looking at it as being unfaithful. Just go for it.''

"Easier said than done.''

The truth was, even as she said that, Della realized she did feel better. She felt as if a huge weight had been lifted from her shoulders. And oddly, as if in remembering what Bucky had said to her on just this subject, both jokingly and not, she also felt as if he'd had a hand in taking that burden off her.

"You deserve to be happy,'' Kansas said firmly. "To have love in your life. To have a man who looks at you the way Yance Culhane looks at you,'' she added with a bit of slyness to that last part.

"Why do you keep saying that? He doesn't look at me any differently than he looks at anyone.''

"Oh, yes, he does. Those beautiful Culhane baby blues light up the minute they spot you. Along with the rest of that incredible face of his.''

"Are you forgetting you're a married woman?'' Della goaded to get some of the heat off herself.

"Never. Or that my Linc is the best-looking guy in the whole world. But Yance is a close second.''

"He is gorgeous, isn't he?'' Della said in barely more than a whisper as if admitting it was one thing but she couldn't do it too loudly.

"Go for it, Del,'' Kansas repeated. "Go for it and don't feel guilty.''

Della made a face and took the sack of crepe paper into the living room.

Could she go for it? she asked herself.

And could she go for it without feeling terribly, terribly guilty the way she had been these past few days?

She didn't know.

She did know that she felt better now than she had. But she couldn't tell if feeling better, feeling as if the burden of guilt had been lifted from her shoulders, was a permanent thing or just something that had temporarily taken a hike, only to return with Yance and all he roused in her.

She'd just have to wait and see.

But one thing was for sure.

She was eager to have him come back from his dinner with Ashley.

And this time the eagerness wasn't tinged with anything else.

Elk Creek had limited choices in the way of restaurants. There was the Dairy King, a fast-food burger bar; the Buckin' Bronco, which was a honky-tonk saloon that served drinks every night but food only one night a week and wouldn't have been appropriate for a nine-year-old even on that one night; and then there was Margie Wilson's Café.

Margie Wilson's Café was the town diner, a homey place in one of the storefronts on Center Street. Inside it was nothing fancy. Booths lined three walls, a lunch counter boxed in the fourth and tables took up the rest of the floor space.

Even though it was hardly an establishment that took

reservations, Yance had called ahead and explained the special occasion. So when he and Ashley arrived, there was a table waiting for them, set off in a corner, covered in a white linen cloth with two tall candles in the middle of it.

A teenage waitress led them to it, wishing Ashley a happy birthday as she seated them. But Ashley seemed to barely hear her as she stared, mesmerized by the elegance of the candles.

"Is this just for us?" she asked in as much awe as if they'd walked into a five-star restaurant.

"Sure is," the waitress confirmed. "Mr. Culhane ordered a special table for a special birthday. That's what he told Margie, and that's what Margie told me to set up."

"This is where my dad used to take me, but we never got a special table," she informed them both.

Yance made a show of helping her off with her coat and pulling out her chair before taking his own seat on the opposite side of the linen cloth. And when the waitress lit the candles between them, Ashley's eyes brightened.

"This is like in the movies," the little girl said breathlessly.

Neither of them needed menus—it wasn't as if anyone in town was unfamiliar with the fare. Yance ordered a rare steak, and Ashley ordered roast beef, mashed potatoes with gravy and asked if she could have French fries rather than a salad.

The waitress looked to Yance at that. "French fries *and* mashed potatoes?"

"Sounds like a good combination to me," he answered.

The young waitress just smiled and left to put in their order with the cook. Then she came back with water glasses and a soda for Ashley, and after that Yance and his date were on their own.

"Have you had a good birthday so far today, Ashley?" he asked her.

"Pretty good. At school they sang to me and we all got a birthday cookie. But there weren't any presents, except the bookmark my teacher gave me. My friends give me presents, but they won't do it till the party tonight when we go home."

"Did you get any presents at all yet?"

"From my mom. I got a doll that eats pretend food and really chews. And April gave me a candy lipstick, and Billy gave me a comic book, and Nic gave me two pennies and a good rock that looks like it's got a face on it."

"Sounds like you've already had a nice day."

"But it's not over 'cause here I am on my special dinner, and then there's the party with ice cream and cake."

Yance smiled at her, but mostly he was smiling at the fact that she seemed to be enjoying her birthday.

The waitress came with their dinners then, and once everything was served and they began to eat, Ashley talked about what kind of cake her mother had made her and who was coming and what gifts she hoped to still get.

Yance listened and commented here and there, but as he looked at her, his mind wandered. Della was reflected in her daughter and so, for the umpteenth time since he'd brought Billy home from his attempt to run away, it was Della who Yance was thinking about.

There was no doubt that Ashley was her daughter even though Ashley's very round face and dark eyes weren't anything like Della's more refined features and luminous green eyes. But there was still a resemblance in the slight point of her chin, around the mouth, in the delicate curve of both their brows, in the creamy smoothness of her skin and in the same silky auburn hair.

And as glad as Yance was to be doing this for Ashley, as much as he was enjoying the child's chatter, he couldn't help longing for the mother to be in her place. For Della to be sitting across from him, talking to him, laughing, telling him stories...

Oh, yeah, a quiet candlelight dinner for just the two of them was a very appealing thought. And afterward maybe they could take a walk so he could hold her hand—without the gloves that had separated them the day before when he'd helped her up out of the snow. Just his bare hand around hers.

And then maybe he'd put his arm across her shoulders and pull her close to his side. Maybe she'd get cold and he'd have an excuse to hold her. Then kiss her the way he'd wanted to so badly that it had been an itch inside him. An itch so strong he hadn't been able to resist it entirely and the previous afternoon had given in enough to kiss her forehead, to breathe in her sweet scent, to have the warmth of that creamy skin against his mouth...

Yance yanked his thoughts out of the path they'd

fallen into all on their own, reminding himself he was out to dinner with Della's daughter and shouldn't be thinking things like that.

But it was part of the pattern that had begun over the past few days—his mind wandering to Della, to images of her and of what he'd like to be doing with her—

"I remember your baby," Ashley said out of the blue just then, definitely pulling him off that other path and throwing a bucket of ice water on him to keep him off it.

"You do?" he asked in surprise.

"Uh-huh. I played with him in the nursery at church sometimes."

Yance did some quick math, realizing that Ashley would have been six when Jeremy died. Jeremy had been two, so Ashley probably had had occasion to be with him in the church nursery on Sundays.

"He was the prettiest baby I ever saw," she said. "And he liked me. He liked it when I'd stick out my tongue and blow raspberries at him like this," she said, demonstrating.

Yance grinned. "I'll bet he did like that."

"I was sad when he got killed."

"Me, too."

"And scared, too. 'Cause I didn't know children could get killed or die. And if Jeremy could, then I was scared I would, too."

"That would be a pretty scary thing, all right."

"I didn't even think 'bout maybe my dad could die, either."

Yance nodded in understanding, unsure what to say

to that. Taking his cue from Ashley, he said, "I was sad when your dad died, too."

"Me, too," she said. But she didn't seem to be sinking into the blues she'd been in the day before in spite of the fact that they were talking about this. It was just as if they were having a matter-of-fact conversation, as if tonight she could better handle the feelings she had.

"It's kinda funny... Well, not funny like a funny joke that makes you laugh or anything. But funny like, you know, other kinda funny, that you were a dad in a family and now you don't have a family anymore, and we're a family that used to have a dad but doesn't have a dad anymore."

"I guess that is kind of funny," Yance agreed.

"Is that why you been comin' over? Pretendin' like we're your family that you don't have anymore?"

Out of the mouths of babes...

Hadn't he thought himself that he should examine his motives to see if that was the case?

But he hadn't. And this wasn't the time or the place for that kind of soul-searching, so he mentally set it aside for the moment and just answered Ashley's questions ambiguously. "There's a lot of reasons I've been comin' over. Is it bad for me to?"

"No! We like it. Well, me and April and Billy and Nic like it. You're fun even when you make us do stuff like shovelin' snow."

He couldn't help himself. He had to ask. "And how about your mom? Do you think she likes it?"

Ashley shrugged. "I don't know. She's been a lot happier since you been comin' over. And she kinda dresses up a little bit more and she's even been curlin' her hair. Do you think that means she likes that you're comin' over?''

"Maybe," he allowed, feeling a rush of pleasure at the idea that Della could be sprucing herself up for him.

"I know she likes that you fixed the drippin' sink and the toilet and the gate and stuff. She was gettin' all worried about how to do it herself."

"Well, now she doesn't have to worry anymore."

"That's good. I don't like it when she worries." Ashley had finished most of her roast beef, mashed potatoes and the last of the French fries she'd drenched in ketchup, so she pushed her plate away just as Yance had shortly before. "Do you think sometime you'll ever take her out to dinner like this?" she asked.

"Would it be bad if I did?" he countered, repeating the question he'd asked earlier about his coming over, concerned slightly that this time the little girl might say yes.

Ashley seemed to ponder it as the waitress removed their plates. "No, I don't guess it would be bad," was the final verdict. "I came out to dinner with you like I used to go with my dad, so I s'pose my mom could come out to dinner with you like she used to go with my dad, too."

"Think she would?" he heard himself ask before he'd even realized the words were going to come out.

Ashley shrugged again. "I dunno. Maybe. Everybody keeps tellin' her she should go out. So maybe she would. If you asked her."

The bill came then and put an end to their dinner. As Yance paid it he wondered at himself, at the level of elation he was feeling over something as simple as consent from one of Della's kids for him to take her out.

It wasn't as if he'd actually asked Della and she'd agreed. This was merely a hypothetical conversation with a nine-year-old, for crying out loud.

And yet it gave him hope.

A lot of it.

Hope that if Della was putting some effort into her appearance on his account, then she might be as attracted to him as he was to her.

Hope that her kids might be able to accept his seeing their mother on a one-on-one basis.

Hope that Della might agree to see him on that one-on-one basis.

Hope that put a bounce in his step as they left Margie Wilson's Café and made him even more eager to get back to Della's house.

Back to Della.

By the time the guests began to arrive, Della and Kansas had the house decorated with streamers of crepe paper, balloons and a huge banner strung across the archway between the living room and dining room that said Happy Birthday, Ashley.

The guests consisted mainly of Ashley's friends and several of their parents who were also invited to stay for cake and ice cream. It made for a full house, and when Yance and Ashley finally returned from their dinner, Della almost didn't see them come in. And she'd been watching for them.

She'd definitely been watching for them.

Not only to start the games for the kids, but also to

test herself. To see if, when Yance was there again, she was still guilt free.

What she wasn't free of when she first set eyes on him as he followed her daughter in the front door, was that surge of excitement and delight that had been her involuntary response to him so often in the past several days.

But when the excitement and delight rushed through her this time, they weren't slowed down by guilt dragging on their tails.

There was still a small remnant, she realized, that she needed to remind herself to shake off, but for once she actually managed that, and found herself just plain thrilled to have him back. To have him in the house. To have him where she could see him. Where she could hear his voice. Where she could be with him.

Well, where she could almost be with him.

As the hostess of the party, she could only be with him from a distance. She was so busy tending to the kids and the games and the food that she barely had a moment to ask if he wanted more cake or coffee or ice cream as she passed him on a run to somewhere else.

It wasn't as if he was left to stand in a corner by himself through it all. There were plenty of men—fathers of the guests—to talk to. But Della couldn't help wishing she had even a few minutes to spare to be with him herself.

Especially since—busy or not—she was acutely aware of him, and each time she caught him looking her way she felt a fresh thrill, a deep desire for her house to be clear of everyone but him.

Which, of course, didn't happen any time soon. And

the longer the evening wore on, the more intense was her anxiety at the thought that he could very well be the first to leave, robbing her of any chance whatsoever to have a moment alone with him.

By nine o'clock the gifts had all been opened, the cake was decimated, the balloons had been popped and Ashley was wearing a cluster of the crepe-paper streamers around her neck like a boa. But adults finally began to round up tired kids and say good-night.

Della didn't linger over long goodbyes, all the while silently willing Yance not to be the next departure.

But it seemed as if he was the one to linger. In fact, as Della saw her guests out, Kansas started to clean up and Yance pitched in to help. So when the last of the revelers was gone and April, Ashley, Billy and Nic had been sent upstairs to bed themselves, it was Della, Yance, Kansas and a very sleepy Danny left downstairs.

"Why don't you take that boy on home?" Della heard Yance suggest to Kansas as Della headed for the kitchen where the work was in progress. "I'll stay and give Della a hand. You'd better go before Danny drops."

Ordinarily Kansas wouldn't have agreed to such a thing. She'd have been intent on staying and would have called Linc at the Buckin' Bronco, and he'd have left the honky-tonk in the hands of his manager while he picked Danny up to take him home to bed.

But as Della joined them, her sister said, "Would you mind, Del?"

"If you take Danny home? No, go ahead."

Had that sounded too eager? Della couldn't be sure

because that's how she felt. Eager just to be alone with Yance.

Then, remembering her manners, she added, "But you don't have to stay and help, either, Yance. You've already done enough. I can't make you clean up the place, too."

"Who said you were *makin'* me do anything?" he asked as he rolled up his sleeves in a clear indication that he was staying no matter what she said.

To Della's delight.

"Well, if that's settled, Danny and I might as well take off," Kansas put in. Then, when Della made a move to walk her out, too, Kansas added, "No, just stay in here with Yance. Danny and I can let ourselves out. 'Night."

Della threw her sister a look that said she didn't appreciate the edge of insinuation in Kansas's tone, but Kansas only smiled at her and left.

Neither Della nor Yance said much while Kansas hurried Danny through putting on his coat and urging him out the front door, but once they'd gone and the house was suddenly quiet, the silence seemed deafening.

"Really, Yance, you don't have to—"

"Good, because I can be a real stinker about things I have to do," he said, stopping her in midsentence. "Now how about I get stuff picked up out in the rest of the house while you put this kitchen in some kind of order?"

"Okay," she conceded, both to his delegation of duties and his insistence on staying. After all, why fight what she was happy to have happening?

Working together, it didn't take them long before the place was cleaned up, the trash was taken out and all signs of the birthday party were disposed of.

The trouble was, Della still hadn't really spent any time with Yance himself. Fretting once more over the possibility that he might leave, she tried to think of some excuse to keep him there.

Even though she'd been offering him food and drink all evening, that was the only thing she could come up with. So, before he could make any move to go, she said, "How about a nightcap?"

He pressed a big hand to his very flat stomach, making it impossible for Della's gaze not to follow. And once it had, it stuck like glue to his midsection and slightly lower—that portion that she had no business whatsoever looking at.

"Are you tryin' to fatten me up?" he asked.

"No way," she said, her tone full of admiration she felt but hadn't intended to relay. Then, forcing some hard-won control, she yanked her eyes upward to his face again and added, "I mean, no, I don't ever try to fatten anybody up."

But it didn't seem to distract him from that first evidence she'd given of how terrific she thought he looked just the way he was. Yance was grinning at her as if he'd somehow been complimented.

"I wouldn't mind sitting for a minute, though," he said then. "Unless you're tired and want to get to bed?"

"No! I'd like you to stay." Too quick. She was getting herself in deeper and deeper and could have bitten off her tongue.

But Yance's grin just widened.

They'd ended up in the kitchen, and he nodded in the direction of the living room. "How about in there?"

"Sure. It's more comfortable."

Della led the way, discovering as she did that she didn't know where to sit once she got there. It was silly, she told herself, but should she take one of the two single chairs where there was no chance of Yance's sitting anywhere near her? Or should she sit on the couch? And how could a grown woman be in a dilemma over such a dumb thing?

But a dilemma it was, and she finally opted for the couch because she couldn't resist just seeing where Yance would sit if she did.

Except that she sat so far on one end that even though he sat on the sofa, too, there was enough room between them for him to angle toward her with one knee on the cushion, his arm stretched across the back, and still keep a full two feet separating them.

Unfortunately...

"Oh," she said suddenly, getting up to retrieve her purse from the table in the entry beside the door and returning to her end-hugging spot on the couch. "I want to pay for the birthday dinner tonight."

Yance frowned at her. "Put that away," he ordered as she took out her wallet. "It's been a long time since anybody but me paid for my dates, and I won't have that changed now."

"But really—"

"Put it away."

His tone brooked no argument, so she did just that.

"But since you brought up money," he went on, "I've been worrying about that. Are you doin' okay in the finances department with Bucky gone?"

There was genuine concern in Yance's tone, so Della knew he wasn't asking out of nosiness and she didn't mind answering.

"We're fine. Bucky had insurance that covered the mortgage and two big policies on himself. Plus there was a trust fund of his that helped make ends meet even before he died, and we still have money coming in from that. So there's nothing to worry about as long as I keep to the budget we always lived on."

"You know if you ever need anything, though—"

"Thanks, but we're fine." And she wanted to change the subject. "So how *was* your dinner with Ashley? Did she behave herself?"

"She was a perfect lady, and I think it went well. I know I enjoyed myself, and it seemed as if Ashley did, too."

"She was pretty wide-eyed over something about candles like in the movies."

Yance explained the arrangements he'd made ahead of time with Margie Wilson for candlelight and the linen tablecloth.

"That was very nice of you," Della said, acknowledging the thoughtfulness that had made the dinner extraspecial for her daughter.

He frowned in a way that beetled his strong brow and waved away her comment. "No big deal. It was just the diner."

"It was a big deal to Ashley. I think she'll remember

it as her first date, and a lot of those to come will have a hard time living up to it.''

"Speaking of dates,'' he said, obviously wanting to change the subject himself now, ''I got your daughter's go-ahead to take you out on one.''

He said that with a note of teasing, but also with a touch of testing, too, as if to see how Della would react.

She reacted with surprise, because surprised was how she felt. ''The go-ahead to take me on a date?''

"Yes, ma'am. Ashley asked if I was ever gonna take you out to dinner the way I was taking her, and when I asked if that would be okay she gave her blessing.''

"She did?''

"She did,'' he confirmed. ''She said if she could go out with me the way she would have gone out with her dad, then so could you. Now all I need to do is convince you,'' he added with a crooked smile.

"Me?'' She hated that she sounded like a dim bulb, but this whole thing had taken her off guard. And so many conflicting emotions were running rampant through her it wasn't easy to know what was going on or how to respond to any of it.

"*Would* you go out to dinner with me? Say Friday night? I know with Halloween being Saturday that you'll be busy, but I thought maybe Friday...''

"Late Friday afternoon is Savannah's baby shower,'' Della said, thinking out loud and hearing regret echoing in her voice. She couldn't miss the baby shower of her best friend. She and Savannah's sister Ivey were giving it. But for a fleeting moment she actually considered it.

"We could make it a late supper,'' Yance persisted.

"I wouldn't mind holdin' off until you had that all wrapped up."

"But it could go on until eight or so," she said as if he didn't know what he was getting into.

He smiled a small, secret smile. "You're worth waiting for, Della."

It was as if his words poured a warm, sparkling liquid directly into her veins, and Della couldn't help a small smile of her own.

"So how about it? Will you go?" he asked.

Could she do that? Could she go out to dinner, on a date, with a man who wasn't Bucky?

She wanted to, she realized. But that old, familiar guilt she'd hoped to have conquered cropped up in full bloom again.

Only now she didn't let it simply have its way with her. Instead, she put some concerted effort into reminding herself of all she and Kansas had talked about. Of what Bucky had said about finding again the kind of happiness they'd shared if one of them lost the other.

Permission. Yance had said Ashley had given hers. Kansas had thought Bucky had given his a long time ago, Della herself had felt as though she'd been freed of the burden of guilt over her feelings and her attraction to Yance. And if the feeling of guilt had been taken away earlier, when she was thinking more rationally, then they could stay away....

And she could take those permissions seriously.

Except that taking them seriously, acting on them and accepting Yance's invitation meant stepping out of the cocoon of her grief. And she wasn't sure she had the courage to do that.

How much courage did it take when it was Yance who was beckoning her out of that cocoon? she asked herself. Every sense she had was urging her to say yes, to go for it, as Kansas had said, to take that step out of the cocoon and back into life.

"Okay," she said quietly, tentatively.

"You'll go?" Now it was Yance who sounded surprised.

"Yes, I'll go."

His answering grin was so broad it was nearly blinding. "Well, I'll be damned," he muttered softly to himself.

Della liked being unpredictable for a change. "Didn't you think I would?"

"All I could do was hope, Del. All I could do was hope." He shook his head, searching her face as if for signs that she didn't really mean what she'd said and might rescind the acceptance at any moment. But when she didn't, he repeated, "I'll be damned."

The grandfather clock in the hallway chimed just then. Eleven times. And as if it was a signal for him to leave, Yance stood to go.

"I didn't know it was so late. I better let you get some rest."

Della just nodded and stood, too, wanting suddenly to be alone. To think about what she'd done. How she felt about it.

Or maybe what she wanted was just to savor it because so far, she only felt good. And excited. And as if Friday was much too far away.

She walked Yance to the door, handing him his coat from the hall tree and feasting on the sight of those wide shoulders shrugging into it. Shoulders she had an inordinate urge to run the palms of her hands over.

But once he had it on, he didn't seem in any hurry to actually leave.

Instead, he turned to face her, settling penetrating blue eyes on her as he shifted his weight onto one hip and folded his arms over the hard expanse of his chest. Then he nodded in the direction of the stairs.

"You know, sending my date to bed so early robbed me of a good-night kiss."

Della laughed at his joke, appreciating the opportunity to release some of the tension she'd been feeling since agreeing to their date for Friday night. "Sorry. But that's what you get for dating a nine-year-old."

"Maybe you could give it to her for me." There was something mischievous in that, and in his expression to go along with it. But Della wasn't sure why.

"If you want me to kiss my daughter on your behalf, I'd be happy to."

"Great."

And just that fast his hands came to her upper arms, and he pecked a quick kiss on her lips.

"Will that one do?" he said with a full measure of that mischief in the grin he flashed down at her.

"Maybe for a nine-year-old," she heard herself banter back more boldly than she ever expected.

Yance laughed a rich, barrel-chested laugh, and didn't seem to notice how shocked Della was at her own words.

Then, surprising her once more, he leaned in and kissed her again. More firmly but still much, much too briefly.

And Della felt the heat of a blush rise into her cheeks at the same moment a delicious warmth seeped in through her pores in response to a kiss that—even though it hadn't been more than a teasing buss—had left an aftershock in her.

"Better?"

"A little," she teased in spite of what felt a bit like a stupor.

He laughed again. "I'll have to try harder Friday night."

Ah, sweet promises...

He let go of her arms then and finally moved to the door. Opening it before he turned, he said, "'Night, Del," and let himself out.

"'Night," she said to the door as it closed behind him.

Neither of those parting kisses had been the kind high-school girls had gossiped about, but they were enough to leave Della light-headed, weak-kneed and longing for more.

And even if there was just a trace of guilt still threatening to ease its way into her thoughts, she didn't let it.

Because she really had stepped out of the cocoon of grief to finally go on with her life.

And right at that moment it felt too good to let anything stop her.

Chapter Five

"**Y**o! Yance! You're about to put that hinge on backward."

Yance stopped short, took a look at what he was doing and realized his brother Clint was right—he was about to put a hinge on backward. His mind just wasn't on his work as he and both his brothers mended the paddock fence that a tree branch had fallen onto under the weight of the early snow. For the most part the snow had melted away, but the damage remained to be fixed.

The gate was wide enough to back a truck and horse trailer through, so it required a man at each end to hold it while Yance replaced the hinges. Cully was to his left, and Clint to his right.

"So, have you told Amy and Randa about the new

baby yet?'' Clint asked Cully as Yance rectified his mistake.

Cully and his wife, Ivey, had invited Clint and Savannah to breakfast that morning to announce that Ivey was pregnant with a child of their own to add to the two daughters Cully had from his first marriage.

''We told 'em last night,'' Cully confirmed. ''They're thrilled. They're already so excited about yours and Savannah's baby coming that they can hardly see straight and now they'll have one of their own—that's what they said.''

Babies—families—were popping up all around him, Yance thought. And for the first time since the death of his wife and son, he found himself wishing for one of those families for himself.

Wishing and wondering if there hadn't been some validity to Ashley's question as to whether or not he might be pretending her family was the one he didn't have anymore.

In the three years since losing Nancy and Jeremy, Yance hadn't been interested in remarrying or having more kids. He'd gotten through his grief, the pain of losing the two people he'd loved most in the world, but even once he was past all that, he still hadn't had any inclination to try to replace them. He hadn't believed he could replace them.

But was it possible that somewhere along the way that had changed?

''Where's your head today, man?'' Clint said as Yance hunkered down to work on the lower hinge and nearly put it on backward, too.

''I think his head's where he'd like the rest of him

to be—over at Della Dennehy's house," Cully answered with a brotherly goad.

"Ah..." Clint chimed in, "have we got somethin' bloomin' over at the Dennehy place?"

"I've just been helpin' out," Yance said mildly.

"Helpin' out and then coming' home to be distracted from your work," Cully added with a nudge of his knee to Yance's shoulder from where he stood nearby.

Yance didn't have to look up to know Cully and Clint were exchanging looks over his head.

"He's been callin' on Della every night this week," Clint offered to further the cause.

"Now which is it? Are you lendin' a helpin' hand there or callin' on Della?" Cully asked. "Because those are two pretty different things. One's just bein' neighborly. But the other..."

"I've been helpin' out," Yance said, refusing to jump at the bait his brothers were using.

"Don't let him kid you," Clint said. "More's goin' on than just helpin' out—I'd bet a week's pay on it. How much helpin' out can she need, anyway? Especially when all that was goin' on over there last night was a birthday party. And he didn't get back here until after eleven o'clock."

"Sounds like more than helpin' out to me," Cully agreed. Then, to Yance he said, "You takin' her to the monster mash at the Buckin' Bronco tonight?"

"No, I'm not." But he was hoping she might be there on her own to give him a way to see her. Their Friday-night date, which he hadn't told anyone about, seemed like years away.

So many years away that he found himself risking

even more of his brothers' teasing by saying to Clint, "But if you got Savannah to persuade her to go—Savannah bein' her best friend and all—I wouldn't mind too much."

Clint and Cully both laughed and hooted and whistled at that just as Yance's two sisters-in-law came out the back door of the house and headed toward them.

"Must have been a good joke," Ivey said as they came nearer.

"Yeah, how about letting us in on it?" Savannah suggested, settling her girth close to her husband. Their baby was due in less than two weeks, and looking at her gave Yance a pang of envy he'd never felt before.

Rather than explaining outright what they'd been making a commotion about, Clint butted Savannah's side with his hip and said, "Do you happen to know if Della is goin' to the monster mash tonight?"

Yance finished the bottom hinge and stood just in time to see Clint nod in his direction to let both women know that it was Yance who wanted the information.

"Della and Yance?" Savannah said in astonishment. Then, to Yance she said, "Are you interested in Della?"

"Just wonderin' if she'll be there tonight is all," Yance answered, downplaying his interest.

"And wonderin' if Savannah could talk her into goin' even if she wasn't plannin' on it," Cully added slyly.

"Della and Yance…" Savannah repeated as if trying it on for size.

Of course, no one had ever known about the crush Yance had had on Della in junior high school, and

Della had been Bucky's girlfriend and wife for so many years that Yance realized that pairing her up with anyone else would take some getting used to by everyone—*if* he managed to get her paired up—so he didn't take offense to his sister-in-law's difficulty coming to grips with the idea.

But finally, after mulling the combination, Savannah brightened up like a child viewing a whole pile of Christmas presents and said, "Wouldn't that be great? Della and Yance."

"Now, don't get carried away and make more of it than it is," Yance felt obliged to say to pull in the reins of what appeared to be a sudden burst of enthusiasm in Savannah. "There's nothin' goin' on. Nothin' likely to come of it. I just wondered if she'd be there tonight. And wouldn't mind if she was."

"Wouldn't mind tryin' to *make* more of it," Cully jabbed.

"Kansas and I have been trying to talk Della into going tonight," Savannah said. "So far she hasn't given us a definite answer, but I'll see what I can do."

Yance couldn't keep up his impervious act forever and smiled at his sister-in-law. "Thanks. I'd appreciate it."

"Should I be subtle or can I say you'd like it if she'd come?"

"No, don't say it that way. I don't want to scare her off. Maybe just say we all thought it would be nice for her to be part of the group."

"But we'll save the seat right next to her for Yance." It was Clint's turn to tease.

"Okay, I'll be subtle," Savannah said, ignoring her husband's comment. "But I just think this is so great!"

Yance grimaced at what had come out of his sister-in-law as almost a squeal and hoped he hadn't started something he'd regret.

Not that he'd regret Della's coming to the festivities most of town would turn out for. He just hoped he didn't live to regret revealing even as much as he had about his feelings for Della.

"Well, we just came out to tell you guys we have your lunch ready," Ivey offered, possibly taking mercy on Yance to distract his brothers with food.

Since the gate repair was finished, the distraction did the trick. After a few test runs of opening and closing it, Cully and Clint each wrapped an arm around their respective wife's waist and started for the house.

Yance followed behind, getting an eyeful of what his brothers had found with the women they loved. And feeling a fresh surge of envy.

But was it just Della he wanted?

Or was it her whole family he was subconsciously thinking to plug into the slot left vacant by the deaths of Nancy and Jeremy?

He wanted Della; there was no doubt about that. He'd been reliving that simple, unpassionate, teasing kiss he'd given her the night before as if it had been more than it was. A lot more. He'd been all het up inside thinking about holding her against him instead of just grabbing her by the arms, wrapping his own arms around her, feeling her breasts pressed to his chest, kissing her for real....

But still, as he followed behind his brothers and their

wives, Ashley's words of the previous evening niggled at him and he couldn't help wondering, too, if it was possible that he was somehow attempting to replace the family he'd lost as easily as he'd just replaced the broken hinges.

And if that was true, how wise was it to pursue? For him? For Della? For her kids?

It didn't seem wise at all.

But wise or unwise, nothing changed the fact that he was itching to see Della again. Itching not to have to wait until Friday. Itching to know what it would be like to hold her in his arms, kiss her...

And he just couldn't make himself reverse what he'd set into motion—trying to get her to the Buckin' Bronco tonight so he could be with her there.

"Is this a conspiracy or what?" Della asked of her two guests that afternoon.

First her sister Kansas had dropped by, and as Kansas sat at Della's kitchen table while Della made tea, Savannah had appeared on her doorstep. Within minutes of the three of them sitting down with tea and cookies in front of them, it was clear to Della that they had the same goal—to get her to agree to go to the monster mash at the Buckin' Bronco that night.

"Not a conspiracy. Just a coincidence. We all want you to go," Savannah said, putting an odd emphasis on *all*.

"I'd be a fifth wheel with so many couples," Della insisted.

"We aren't *all* couples," Savannah said with more of that odd emphasis.

"You and Clint, Ivey and Cully, Kansas and Linc, Jackson and Ally, Beth and her husband—"

"And Yance," Savannah contributed.

"And you," Kansas added.

Della frowned at them both. "Is this a matchmaking thing?" she asked. She hadn't told anyone—not even Kansas or Savannah—that Yance had invited her out to dinner for Friday night. For some reason the thought of announcing it seemed embarrassing. Besides, she liked keeping the information to herself for the time being, savoring the anticipation before letting anyone else in on it.

Kansas and Savannah denied in unison that they were playing matchmaker, but Savannah's denial was a little too vehement and made Della wonder if Yance himself hadn't sent her on this errand.

Which put a whole different light on the coming evening.

"We'll be together," Kansas said. "And that's too many people to be a couples' deal. We'll just be a group."

"And you'll be part of that group," Savannah added.

Part of a group with Yance...

But also part of a group she'd always been in with Bucky.

"I don't have a baby-sitter," she said to avoid the strangeness that seemed inherent in that situation.

"You can always call Heather next door. The kids will be ready for bed before you leave, so all she'll need to do is tuck them in, sit and watch TV—just what she'd be doing at home anyway. We have Stevie

Johnson staying with Danny, and he can't wait. Kids love teenage baby-sitters,'' Kansas persisted.

"And you deserve a night out," Savannah added.

Della bit back saying that she was getting a night out on Friday.

"Come on, Del, come with us," Kansas urged.

"It wouldn't be the same without you."

Just as it wouldn't be the same for Della without Bucky....

On the one hand she was tempted, she had to admit. But on the other hand she was equally reluctant. If she went to the Buckin' Bronco that night, it would be the first time she'd been to any Elk Creek social, kick-up-her-heels kind of event since his death. The first without him.

And somehow that seemed more difficult to come to grips with than a quiet dinner alone with Yance on Friday night. This would be exactly the way she'd spent any number of evenings before, with exactly the same people. Minus Bucky.

But with Yance...

Torn. She was torn.

"I don't think so," she said, her cold feet getting the better of her suddenly.

"Because of Bucky," Kansas surmised, reading Della like a book. "You can't stay away from everything you guys would have ever done together because he's not here anymore, Del. Are you going to spend the rest of your life sitting out Thanksgiving and Christmas and Easter and the Memorial Day celebrations and the Fourth of July, and Labor Day and the Harvest Festival and everything that's fun that you once did with Bucky rather than face doing them without him now?''

''I've already gone through a whole year full of those kinds of things without sitting out any of them—well, there was no Harvest Festival in Phoenix.''

''Which is exactly the point—you went through the motions in Arizona with Mom and Dad. That's different than doing any of it here, where you did it all with Bucky for so long. I think you're afraid if you do the things you did with him before—or things like the monster mash that you *would* have done with him—in the old, familiar places with the old, familiar faces, it'll bring back too many memories. But you have to do it, have the memories and get through it, to ever be able to go on.''

''Have you been reading some kind of grief-counseling book or something?'' Della asked her sister, making a joke out of what Kansas was being very serious about, what seemed like the second verse of the advice she'd given the previous evening over the guilt Della had been suffering.

''It's just common sense,'' Kansas said.

''It's true, though,'' Savannah interjected. ''And at least if you go, you'll have all our old, familiar faces to support you and help you get through the hard feelings.''

''If they come up. Which they might not. Or they might not be as bad as you think they will,'' Kansas said. Then, in a lighter tone of her own and with a smile that didn't seem able to be kept down, she added, ''And Yance will be there.''

Savannah smiled, too, much the way Kansas did—

as though she couldn't suppress it. "Does that make a difference to you? That Yance will be there?"

Before Della could answer, Kansas said, "She has a little bit of an eye for him."

Savannah leaned as far over as her massively pregnant stomach would allow and said in a confidential tone, "He has a little bit of an eye for you, too."

"See? I told you so," Kansas said with a laugh. "Now, come on, say you'll go tonight. I promise you that we'll make it as painless as possible, and once you're over this first hurdle you won't have to hide out to avoid things like this. You'll be able to enjoy them again."

"And you don't even have to wear a costume if you don't want to."

"It would probably be easier to find a costume than to find something in my closet that fits," she heard herself say, sounding as if she were agreeing to go before she'd actually made up her mind.

But she knew why. She knew it was the temptation of Yance, of getting to see him again before Friday night, that was pulling her, and was winning the tug of war with her reluctance to put herself in a situation she would have only been in before with Bucky.

"Then you'll go?" This from Savannah, in a hopeful tone.

"She'll go," Kansas responded with finality, as if Della had said she would. "Because I won't let her not go."

But Della didn't say too much at all. She was lost in her own thoughts, in the feelings warring inside her.

Feelings that ranged from dread to delight and back again.

But in the end the delight won out, and she let her sister push her that last distance to agreement because it meant she'd be with Yance.

She just hoped being with Yance—and not being with Bucky—in one of those old, familiar places, with so many other old, familiar faces, was a transition she could make.

The honky-tonk was already hopping by the time Kansas had picked up Della and they got to the establishment Kansas's husband owned and operated. Linc had advertised the evening as a little pre-Halloween fun for the adults of Elk Creek, and apparently that idea had a wide appeal.

Costumes were optional, but almost no one there was without one. Some were elaborate, like Cully's and Ivey's Robin Hood and Maid Marian, and another couple who came as Darth Vader and Princess Leia. Most were less elaborate and more ordinary—there was a fair share of rabbits, bears, gorillas, clowns, hobos and hippies. There was one Charlie Chaplin. But the majority of the costumes were very simple, like Della's last-minute concoction. She was wearing black slacks and a black tunic onto which she'd stuck a plethora of the silver stars she ordinarily used as recognition for her children's accomplishments.

Kansas had come dressed as a dance-hall girl to go with Linc's Doc Holliday getup; Savannah and Clint were matching pumpkins—about the only thing that would accommodate Savannah's current shape; Beth

Heller and her Native American husband, Ash Black-wolf, came as an Indian brave and his squaw; Jackson Heller's wife, Ally, had been a chef in Denver before arriving in Elk Creek and she came in her chef's coat and hat, while Jackson was done up as a giant turnip and good-naturedly took a great deal of ribbing for it.

And then there was Yance.

As Kansas led the way to the table that all the Hellers and the Culhanes were sharing, Della followed behind, scanning faces masked and unmasked to locate him.

She spotted him at the bar, talking to Linc. Yance was a stark contrast to Linc's all-black attire. He was dressed in an old-fashioned white suit with a black ribbon tie, a white hat tipped to one side and a cigar the size of a carrot jammed into the hatband.

He looked rakish and dashing and, to Della, like the most handsome man in the room, helping to block out the déjà vu she was suffering walking into the Buckin' Bronco for the first time without her husband.

The minute Yance caught sight of her, he ended his conversation with Linc and headed through the crowd to the huge round table, maneuvering himself to the chair beside the one Della was about to take for herself.

"Happy Halloween—almost," he said, making it sound as if he were greeting more than just Della but keeping his glorious blue eyes fixed on her alone the whole while.

"Happy Halloween—almost," she answered.

He bent over slightly as if to tell her a secret and said, "In case you hadn't guessed, I'm a riverboat gambler."

"Hmm. I thought you were Mark Twain," she teased him when a riverboat gambler was what she'd been thinking all along.

"Are you seein' white hair and a big bushy mustache somewhere?" He feigned insult.

"No, now that you mention it, I guess I don't."

"A gambler. I'm a gambler," he reiterated.

"At heart or just for tonight?" she teased him.

"These days it's lookin' like I might be one at heart. Or at least that I might be gamblin' *with* my heart," he said, arching his eyebrows.

He studied her openly for a moment before those brows turned puzzled. Then he said, "You're gonna have to clue me in here, Del. What are you?"

"Not a gambler," she said with a laugh.

"Could be we can change that. But what I meant was, what's your costume? Or is this a new fashion statement?"

"I'm the night sky," she told him matter-of-factly.

That made him chuckle lightly as he reared back and gave her the once-over from head to toe to head again. "You're lookin' a little baggy, Night Sky," he teased, but kindly, and with just enough appreciation in his voice and in his expression to take any sting out of it. "Can I get you a drink?"

Della was wound as tightly as a drum and although she wasn't much of a drinker, she hoped a glass of wine might help her relax. So she accepted the offer and watched him wend his way back to the bar, wishing his suit coat weren't as long as it was because it blocked the most enticing part of his rear view and left her with only a wide white expanse of shoulders to feast on.

Compliments, explanations and jokes about costumes filled the time until Yance got back. No sooner had he sat beside Della again than the band that had been setting up on the stage that occupied the wall opposite the bar tested their microphones and kicked off the music with a loud blast of a country two-step.

Yance handed Della her wine and moved close enough for his voice to be heard over the din. "Would you like to dance?"

Della hadn't been doing too badly up to that point. Yes, it had seemed strange not to have Bucky nearby, not to have him at her elbow or within the sound of her voice, but his absence hadn't been as glaring as she'd worried it might be.

Yet dancing was something else entirely.

Della and Bucky had both loved it and would have seized the opportunity of a night like this to dance until their feet ached.

And somehow she couldn't bring herself to walk out onto the floor just below the stage and share that with another man.

Not even if that other man was Yance. And not even though she'd danced with plenty of other men when Bucky had been alive. She just couldn't do it.

"No, thanks. I think I'll sit this one out," she said, thinking about her sister's using just that phrase that afternoon. It might have helped get her to the Buckin' Bronco but it couldn't get her as far as dancing.

Nothing could, even as the night wore on and every man at their table—as well as a few from other tables—

tried. Della thanked each one for asking, but refused to set foot on that dance floor.

She had a surprisingly good time anyway, though. And that was thanks to Yance. He stayed close by to joke with her and flirt with her and make sure her wineglass was always full.

In fact, he only left her side to replenish drinks, asking a few more times for a dance but never pushing it, keeping her laughing with a running commentary on the costumes around them and what they said about the people wearing them, and never leaving her too long to look around and find herself alone among the sea of couples.

At the stroke of ten o'clock a signal from Linc halted the band's playing. The abrupt silence muted the room, and the lead singer stepped up to the mike to tell what, at first, seemed like just any old story. But the story proved to be the headless horseman, and the longer the singer went on, the more eerie turned his tone of voice.

Then, at just the right moment, the great doors and all the cattle doors around the building—which had once been a holding barn—were thrown open at once and outside, riding around and around the Buckin' Bronco on a coal black stallion was what looked to be that very headless horseman.

Nearly everyone in the place flooded out those doors to see the sight as inside the singer finished the tale with a bang. Again, with perfect timing the headless horseman made off into the night.

A roar of hoots and hollers and applause went up before the music started once more and the crowd found its way back inside.

Everyone but Della, who stayed to cool off in the clear, chilly air that felt so good after the heat of too many people and too much smoke in one place.

Everyone but Della and Yance, who also lingered when he saw that Della wasn't returning with the rest.

"Hot?" he guessed, his deep voice wafting through the quiet that was suddenly left with all the revelers gone back to their tables and even the music dimmed by all the doors closed after them.

"Mmm. It just seemed so nice out here that I thought I'd steal another minute or two of it before I go in. I'm fine, though—you don't have to baby-sit me."

"Is that what I'm doing? Baby-sitting you?"

"I don't know. Is it? You haven't gone off to have much fun the whole night."

"Gone off to have fun?" He shook his head as if he didn't believe she could be so blind. "I've been havin' fun. This was just what I wanted tonight. It was me who put Savannah up to that visit she made to you today to get you here tonight in the first place. And not so I could do any baby-sitting."

That made Della smile. Both because she'd been right about Savannah's intentions and because Yance had put effort into seeing her tonight. It was flattering. And it pleased her to no end.

"I just thought my old friend wanted my company," she lied.

"I'm sure she did. But so did I."

"Why didn't you just ask for it, then?"

That seemed to take him aback. "You mean you would have come with me tonight if I had? Out on a date in front of everybody?"

"No," she answered honestly, with another laugh. "I probably wouldn't have. Not here, tonight, with the whole town looking on and everybody else coupled up. It'll be different Friday night. That's just dinner between two separate people."

"That's what I thought. So I took a different tack. And this one worked better because here you are."

Della let her head fall back so she could gaze up at the stars in the clear autumn night. "And here I am," she said, glad she was.

"Here you are, lookin' at the night sky to see if you match up, and drinkin' a little wine, and seeming as if you're having a pretty nice evening."

"I am having a pretty nice evening."

"Except that you haven't danced a lick. Della the dancin' fool hasn't had a single spin around the floor."

Della just went on staring up at the stars, not responding to that.

But even when it was obvious that she wasn't going to, Yance wouldn't let it drop. "How come, Delaware?" he asked enticingly. "How come you came tonight and you've let me sit with you and talk to you and tease you, but you won't let me dance with you? What're you afraid of? That I'll step on your toes?"

That made her smile. "No, I'm not afraid you'll step on my toes. I've seen you dance. You're good at it."

"So you're afraid you'll step on mine, then?"

"I beg your pardon." She pretended to be offended, finally looking straight at him with the intention of giving him a withering glance. But somewhere up the long length of him that idea fizzled. Instead, she just ended up being bowled over by the fact that he was standing so nearby, tall and straight and towering above her, a pillar of pure, potent masculinity.

Yance caught and held her eyes with his, looking deeply into them, probing them.

"For a while I thought maybe you might be afraid that you'd be bein' unfaithful to Bucky if you took to the floor," he said. "I remembered not eating chocolate-chip ice cream for more than a year because Nancy and I had eaten it together so many times it seemed terrible for me to be able to go on enjoying something she'd never have again. Something we'd never be able to share. Seemed like cheatin' somehow."

"Maybe I just didn't feel like dancing tonight," Della said as if he hadn't come dangerously close to at least a part of what was going on with her.

"Your foot's been tappin' up a storm this whole evening."

Caught in the act.

But still she felt foolish about the real reason, so she couldn't tell him what it was. She could only tell him what it wasn't. "It isn't that I'd feel like I was being unfaithful. I would have danced with other men when Bucky was alive and not have been cheating, so it wouldn't have seemed that way tonight."

"I thought about that, too," he confided. "So then I did some more thinking about what it might be that was keeping you from doing what we all know you love to do, wonderin' if it might just be me you didn't want to dance with."

"It definitely isn't you," she was quick to assure. "I can't believe you thought it was."

He shrugged with mock self-deprecation. "How

could I be sure of that before you turned down everybody else, too?''

''But I *did* turn down everybody else, too,'' she said, sounding more coy than she'd intended to. What she'd wanted to do was just make light of this subject that wasn't, and to escape the sense that Yance could see too far beneath the surface of her. But neither of those things was accomplished, and instead she ended up feeling like a flirtatious teenage girl. An ineptly flirtatious teenage girl.

But Yance didn't seem to notice. Or to be put off by it if he did. He just said, ''Okay, so you know it would be crazy to feel unfaithful to Bucky if you tripped the light fantastic with someone other than him, and you don't find me too repulsive. Then how about it? Will you dance with me out here under the stars?''

''No, thanks, I just don't feel—''

He raised a single, thick index finger and pressed it to her lips to cut short her refusal, shaking his head at her. ''You just don't *want* to feel, is the truth of it. That's what's really going on here tonight, isn't it? You're afraid that if you do something you did so much of with Bucky—only now you do it with someone else—what might happen is that even for just a minute you might forget it *isn't* Bucky you're dancin' with. And that'd hurt.''

Della couldn't admit to it outright. But Yance had stumbled across the answer.

Yet the confirmation must have been there in her expression for Yance to see as he went on searching her face, holding her eyes in the warm, understanding embrace of his, because he smiled a crooked, almost shy smile and said, "I had an experience like that a while after Nancy had passed on, but it was in a more delicate situation than dancin'."

Della smiled, imagining him in a situation more delicate than dancing and forgetting in the middle of it that his partner wasn't his wife. But it was heartening to see that he could look back on it now with amusement.

He nodded just barely in the direction of the great doors that were not far away and from which the refrains of a slow song could barely be heard. "Dance with me, Della," he said so, so softly.

Tempting. It was very tempting....

"Oh, I don't know..."

"*I* know," he said with confidence as he took her elbow in one strong hand and turned her to face him. Then he clamped her right hand in his, placed her left on his shoulder and let his left slide down to her waist.

But he didn't start the dance right then. Instead, he still honed in on her eyes with those spectacular blue eyes of his as he said, "Keep watchin' my face so you remember whose arms you're in."

And then he took the first few steps of a slow country waltz, holding her far enough away for their gazes to stay locked but not so far away that she didn't feel as if he was holding her. Holding her as gently as if she were made of blown glass but with a firmness that let her know he was there, that he could lead her through this dance and more than this dance, that he could lend support and still catch her if she fell—physically and emotionally. That he was there for her in any way she needed or wanted him to be.

And emotionally it *was* difficult for Della.

Even looking at Yance's handsome face didn't make it easy not to think of Bucky, of dancing just that way with her husband. Under the stars. Late at night.

Before Kansas had met Linc, Kansas would always herd the kids home so Della and Bucky could have the last dance of occasions like this. So that, no matter how hectic the festivities had been, how scattered their attention, for that last dance Della and Bucky had been able to come together again and put everything else aside to share one final, romantic moment to end the evening. One final, romantic moment alone together, reconnecting in a way they had both had a particular fondness and talent for, especially when they were in each other's arms...

Della had loved that man. Loved him with all her heart. Loved dancing with him. Loved being in his arms.

But he wasn't there anymore. He'd never be there again. And oddly enough, the longer she went on dancing with Yance, looking up into those moon-kissed features in all their masculine perfection, the more thoughts of Bucky began to fade into the background all on their own.

It was almost as if Bucky himself were stepping back, stepping so far back that he was giving way to Yance. To Yance's having a place there with Della. *His* place with Della. The place that Bucky would never again occupy.

And little by little, Della felt her focus changing. Felt Bucky move to the rear of her thoughts, to take a space only in memory while Yance was right there before her. Flesh and blood. Hard muscle and bone. Steely strong and steady. Peering down at her the way she'd thought no other man ever would again.

And she was relishing it just as she'd relished it when Bucky had looked at her like that. She was feeling it seep in through her pores to warm her from the inside out, to chase away a private chill she'd had for more than a year now.

"How're you doing, Del?" he asked in a tender voice.

"Good. This is nice," she said so tentatively it was clear it had taken her by surprise to find it true.

His answering smile couldn't have been more pleased, more satisfied.

"Were you kissing someone when you forgot it wasn't Nancy, or doing something even more delicate?" she asked then, because curiosity got the better of her.

"I'd already kissed her—but nothing more delicate than that. Except that I was holdin' her, enjoyin' just a minute of closeness with someone soft and feminine, enjoyin' the smell of somethin' better than my brothers and horses, cows, pigs and manure. I shut my eyes for just a minute, and that's when it happened. I blocked out who was really in my arms and called her Nancy," he explained with more of that wry humor in his tone.

"Bet that put an end to that."

"Real quick."

Yance pulled Della nearer then and said, "Think you can handle this now?"

Being pressed up against that long, hard man's body felt too good not to try. "I think so."

And amazingly enough she did just fine. Yance's presence was so powerful, and that image and those memories of Bucky had receded so sharply that she didn't for a moment lose her grip on who was so expertly guiding her in that dance. She was acutely aware of whose arms were around her; whose hard, broad chest her cheek was against; whose chin rested atop her head; whose clean-scented aftershave was filling her senses; whose giant shoulder she held in one hand; whose bulging biceps her other palm curved around....

"Thank you," she whispered because she was grateful for his easing her through this transition, because he'd taken the time and trouble to give back to her something she'd enjoyed and had feared she might never be able to enjoy again. And because she felt so relaxed, so cared for, so cherished at that moment.

"Don't thank me," Yance said, his deep voice letting her know there was as much in that dance for him as there was for her.

And then he raised his chin from the top of her head.

Della thought he had something more he wanted to say, so she glanced up at his chiseled face.

"Keep your eyes open if you need to," he said just before he lowered his lips to hers, taking her by surprise.

Though not so much surprise that she pulled away.

No, she stayed where she was. She arched her neck to help further the cause. And she did leave her eyes open. Open to see the beauty of this man inside and out.

But she didn't keep them open long. This was not Bucky; there was no doubt about it whether she was looking at Yance or not. And yet kissing him at that moment seemed as natural as any kiss she'd ever shared with her husband. As right. As destined. So she let her lids drift down, let herself accept the kiss that was nothing at all like the teasing pecks of before. Nothing at all like any she'd shared with Bucky.

It was the kind of kiss that had earned Yance—and his brothers after him—the reputation that no female had really been kissed until they'd been kissed by a Culhane. His lips were just soft enough, just firm enough and parted just far enough. He knew the perfect pressure to be masterful but not intimidating. To take command and lead yet not to overpower. And when he kissed her, it was as if he was so totally involved that every part of him enveloped her in a delicious, intoxicating sensation that Della could have indulged in for hours and hours and hours....

Except that just then a group of people came out the honky-tonk's great doors, and that ended it.

But somehow that kiss stayed with her all the way back into the Buckin' Bronco. All through the last half hour she spent there, once more surrounded by an abundance of friends and relatives with Yance attentively by her side.

It stayed with her all through the drive home with Kansas when they called it a night. All through Della's absentmindedly washing her face and climbing into her bed.

Because that dance Yance had led her into, led her through, and that kiss he'd given had told her something about herself.

It had told her with indisputable vigor that she was

still alive. That she was still a young woman with healthy desires.

And that a man who wasn't Bucky could awaken all those desires in her once again and make her feel good. Great. Better than great.

It told her that Yance could make her feel wonderful.

And even though she was one day closer to Friday and having dinner with him, somehow it seemed even further away than it had before.

Because she craved so much more of the feelings he'd stirred in her tonight.

So much more time with him.

So much more of him.

And the craving was so strong she wasn't sure she could wait for it to be soothed.

Chapter Six

"Okay. That takes care of that. Now for you."

It was about ten the next morning, and Della squinted at her sister as her eyes adjusted to the bright autumn sunshine they'd just stepped out into from the dimmer confines of Elk Creek's maternity and baby-furnishings shop. Savannah's baby shower was the next afternoon, and they'd been shopping for her gifts, using to their advantage the time when Della's four kids and Kansas's stepson, Danny, were all in school.

"Now for me?" Della repeated, confused.

"Let's do some shopping for you. For clothes that fit."

"Oh, we don't need to do that."

Kansas looked her up and down, let out a "Ha!" and said, "Yes, we do need to do that. You're beginning to look clownish, and I've been worried all morning that your pants are going to fall down around your ankles.''

Della didn't take offense to the criticism. She knew it was true. And the idea of new things was very enticing. Especially when she thought about her date the following evening with Yance—the date she hadn't yet told her sister about.

Still, Della was a frugal person who, except in rare instances of pure necessity, used the clothing allowance on things for the kids—who *always* needed something.

''Maybe I could take a few tucks—''

''Tucks? In blue jeans? That would look worse than clownish. Face it, Del, you need new clothes.''

Considering that she needed them helped. But she hesitated anyway. ''My things are still good, though. There aren't any holes in my jeans or snags in my sweaters or balls on my knits or anything.''

''If your clothes are still in good shape, then give them to charity so somebody they fit can have them. But they don't fit you anymore, and whether they have holes or balls or snags or not, you *need* new stuff.''

Della considered that standpoint.

But before she could consider it for too long, Kansas said, ''When the kids outgrow their clothes you don't hesitate to put them in new ones, whether it be hand-me-downs from the older kids or something new. This is the same thing. Except that you haven't gotten too big for your things—they've gotten too big for you.''

It made sense. And pushed Della nearer to what felt like an indulgence no matter how she looked at it.

''Maybe a few things,'' she finally conceded. And then she decided to confide in her sister. ''I could get a couple of pairs of jeans, maybe a sweater or two, and I do need something to wear to go to the shower tomorrow afternoon and out to dinner afterward."

Kansas looked at her as if she hadn't heard her correctly. "Out to dinner?"

"With Yance."

"With Yance?" Kansas said loudly enough to draw stares.

"Shh…"

"When did this happen? Last night? While you two were outside alone for so long?"

Della shook her head. "He asked me after the birthday party night before last. He talked me into it, really. He said Ashley had given him the okay and, well, he's a persuasive guy."

Kansas's shock turned into an ear-to-ear grin. "You have a date," she said as if it was the cutest thing she'd ever heard.

It made Della cringe to have someone say it out loud, particularly as if Kansas were the proud parent and Della her daughter announcing she'd been asked to the prom. "We're just going out for a little supper after the shower. I'll already have a sitter at home for the kids while I'm at the shower anyway and I'll be right there at the Culhanes' house, and I'll have to eat. It'll just be two friends having a meal together."

"It's a date and you know it. And I can't believe you didn't call to tell me the minute you accepted."

"It's just not that big a deal." *Liar, liar, pants on fire…*

Kansas linked her arm through Della's and headed them both across Center Street to the boutique—the only option for women's clothing besides the sweat suits Kansas stocked in the general store Linc was minding for her today.

"I'm so excited for you," Kansas gushed.

And this time Della didn't deny that there was reason for that excitement.

She just couldn't without feeling like a hypocrite.

Because, as if receiving such tacit approval for the date had released it full bore, no matter how excited Kansas was for her, Della was a hundred times more excited for herself.

Once she got started, Della bought more than she'd intended to. A lot more, she realized later that afternoon when she had all the kids home from school and started to empty the sacks full of clothes, underwear and even a new bottle of perfume Kansas had talked her into. In fact, she'd purchased so much that there was no way she had enough free hangers or closet space to just add the new things to the old. That meant the old were going to have to be boxed up and donated to charity—as Kansas had suggested—to make room for the new.

Della was surprised to find her hands slightly shaky as she took those first few articles from her closet. Most of her clothes had been around a long time. She'd grown accustomed to them. They were like the stuffed rabbit Billy had to have to go to sleep at night—security. And they were definitely part of her life with Bucky, part of the woman she'd been with him.

It wasn't easy folding up the red dress he'd always liked so much. Or the T-shirt he'd slipped off one Sunday afternoon when the kids were all napping to make memorable love to her on the sofa. There were the jeans he'd liked to slide his hands into the back pockets of. The jumper he'd joked made her look like a schoolteacher. The silk blouse he'd bought for her two Christmases ago...

When she pulled that out of the closet, she almost decided she couldn't go through with this. She almost put back every single piece of clothing she'd taken out and resacked the new things to return to the store.

Almost.

But not quite.

Instead, she sat down on the edge of her bed with the silk blouse in her hands and looked from the old to the new to the old again.

The old clothes didn't fit by four or five sizes. It would be ridiculous to keep them and return the new things that actually did fit. Yet she knew that she was not only saying goodbye to some of her—and Bucky's—favorite things, to things that held sweet memories of the two of them together, but that she was also saying goodbye to some of her past, to a life she didn't lead anymore, a part of herself that no longer existed.

And the funny thing about it was that even as that made her unbearably sad, she also felt something else alongside it. It was as if saying goodbye to it all had a cathartic effect, too, allowing a kind of peace to settle over her. Peace, a strong feeling of that excitement she and Kansas had talked about that afternoon and a nice sense of anticipation for ushering in what would now be her future. A future that suddenly didn't look too bad to her.

That was due, in no small part, to Yance, she realized as his image popped into her mind just then.

Because since Yance had come onto the scene, since he'd been teasing and flattering and pursuing and easing her into that future, she'd been looking ahead at what was to come more than she'd been looking backward at days gone by.

It surprised her to recognize that, but it was true. Moments like this one when she thought of Bucky, missed him, relived things they'd shared, were becoming fewer, while thoughts of seeing Yance again, being with him, wondering what he might say or do next, where they might be headed—these were taking up the lion's share of her ponderings.

She really was moving on, she realized.

And as sad as she could still be over having lost the man she'd loved most of her life, there were more times that she didn't feel sad or empty or alone anymore. Rather, she felt hopeful and happy and even excited about what might be around the next bend—

"Can we wear our costumes tonight?"

Della jumped a foot at the sound of Billy's voice coming from the doorway.

"You scared me to death," she said with a laugh at herself and how deeply she'd been lost in her own thoughts. "What did you say?"

"Can we wear our costumes tonight to the haunted house?"

"No, the costumes are just for trick-or-treating Saturday night. Tonight we'll go in regular clothes. But I think they're having face painting and if you kids want to do that, you can. That'll be sort of like having on a costume.''

That seemed to satisfy her son, who charged off down the hall, leaving Della to the task at hand and her thoughts once again.

But more to the task than the thoughts.

She stood up from the bed and went back to folding the large-size clothes to set in the charity box and putting the smaller ones on the hangers that remained behind.

''Off with the old, on with the new.''

In more ways than one.

Every year Elk Creek's PTA put on an elaborate haunted house. Several classrooms and hallways were designated for it and draped in mazes of black canvas tunnels that began at the rear entrance to the school. A two-headed ghoul guarded the Gates of Hades, where he warned in an ominous growl that this was not for the fainthearted.

It was Nic's first year to be allowed to go, and he clung to Della's hand in a viselike grip even as he insisted he was big enough not to be afraid. Della wasn't worried about it. She'd been there often enough before to know that anywhere it got particularly gruesome there was a red warning light and an alternate route so smaller kids or squeamish adults could go on to tamer displays.

And most everything was relatively tame, done all in good fun, so that it turned out to be more cartoonishly frightening than actually terrifying.

Spiderwebs and diaphanous ghosts, dancing skeletons and treasure chests with skulls among the gold doubloons were the first few things they passed, and Nic relaxed enough to let go of his mother's hand and get into the spirit of things.

Cackling, warty-nosed, green-skinned witches reached out from the sidelines with clawed fingers that came just short of grasping them as they traveled the path through the haunted house.

A madman wielding a hatchet threatened anyone who ventured near him. Ravens with shiny red eyes caw-cawed at them. A werewolf rattled the cage he was in, making a horrible racket as he pretended to try to break out. An evil-looking hunchback attempted to persuade passersby to release him from his chains. A cyclops demanded the kids do a trick in order for them to pass.

There were spiders aplenty, ominous owls and wild-eyed cats that were all skin and bones. Dracula bit a fainting teenager's jugular in one corner. Frankenstein walked like a zombie across a fork in the road to let only the bravest into the area from which screams of the tortured and damned drifted out. And around the last bend the creature from Black Lagoon jumped out of the shadows for a grand finale that got everyone's adrenaline pumping.

About that time Nic grabbed Della's hand once more, though out of reflex not fear, because by then it was clear he was enjoying himself as much as the rest of the kids were.

And then they spilled out into the gymnasium, where games were set up for the younger participants to win prizes. Food and drinks were available in the cafeteria that was connected to it, and Nic let go of his mother's hand again in a hurry lest his brother see it and make fun of him.

As with so many of the activities in Elk Creek, there was a good showing. Both the gym and the cafeteria were brimming with people when Della and the kids got to that point.

Not everyone had chosen—as Della had—to attend the festivities in street clothes. Many adults in particular had come in costume, so the crowd presented as interesting a sight as the costumed folks who were running things.

One such monster-masked man came up behind Della as she and the kids stepped from the haunted house into the gym and held out a plastic severed hand.

"One of you lose this?" he asked in a doofus voice.

The kids all laughed and said, "Ooh, ick."

Then Billy pulled his sleeve down over his own hand, held up what was meant to appear to be a stump and said, "I think I did."

"Here you go, then." The man gave the plastic hand to Billy, pulled a rubber squeak toy shaped like a human foot out of his back pocket and said, "How about this?"

April giggled and accepted that one.

Next came a hairy tarantula that Billy wanted more than the severed hand so he shoved the hand off onto Nic and snatched up the spider. Then a pair of glasses with eyeballs springing from the lenses came from the man's shirt pocket, and after trying them on over the mask, he handed them to Ashley, telling her she was an eye popper. "Like her mama," he added slyly.

The kids were delighted by him, and amid their laughs and some spider sound effects from Billy—who was trying to be menacing—Nic said, "Is that Uncle Linc in there?"

"Uh…nope," the man answered, bending over to tickle his inquisitor.

Each child took a turn guessing while Della stood by and watched, enjoying the scene and the fun the masked man was creating for her kids.

But she didn't have to guess who he was. She'd known the moment she glanced up at the monster mask that looked more goofy than scary with its tongue hanging out the side of its rubbery mouth and its wild-hair brows sticking out every which way.

There was no mistaking the blazing blue eyes peering out from behind the sockets. And even if she hadn't recognized Yance's eyes, she'd have known his tall, powerful body. It wasn't a body to go with the silly face of the mask by any means.

"I know who you are," Ashley finally said, sounding confident. "You're Yance!"

"Ah, you found me out," he pretended to lament, pulling the mask up to reveal that drop-dead gorgeous face hidden behind it.

He took the mask completely off, put it on the top of Nick's head like a hat and then ran both his hands through his own short-cropped hair.

Between the mask—which had gone all the way over the top of his head—and the finger combing, his hair stood up at odd angles. Maybe the way he looked first thing in the morning, Della thought, enticed by the possibility. And yet even mussed hair didn't do a single thing to detract from the man's appeal. In fact, she found him all the more attractive looking disheveled and sexy....

"See? I told you it was Yance," Ashley said victoriously.

"I knew it, too. I was just playin' along," Billy claimed, clearly having had no idea who was really behind the mask but unwilling to be outwitted by his sister. "Can we go have our faces painted now?" he asked before anyone could refute his assertion. "I'm gonna have 'em do it like a brick wall so's I can blend in and spy on people an put my spider on 'em when they don't know it's me."

"Me, too," Nic chimed in more because he had a need to seem as grown-up as his big brother than because he wanted to do the same thing.

Then the girls opted for the face painting, too, and as the kids ran in that direction, Della didn't have any choice but to follow them.

With Yance keeping her company.

"What are you doing here tonight?" she asked him, her pleasure in the fact that he was there echoing in her voice so the question didn't come out sounding as tactless as it might have.

"I heard you tell Kansas last night that you were bringin' the kids here this evenin'. It sounded like fun, so I thought I'd give it a try. I went through the haunted house right behind you guys. That all right?"

The rakish smile he tossed her way was much too charming to resist.

"As far as I know, anybody who wants to and has the price of admission can go through the haunted house, so sure, it's all right." Actually it was a lot more than all right with her that he'd shown up tonight, but it wouldn't do to let him know that. "I'm just surprised that this is something you'd want to come to."

"With you and those kids of yours here? Can't think of anything I'd rather be doing."

As if to prove it, he joined the kids at the face-painting table, took one of the brushes that was there for anyone who wanted to do it themselves and pointed it at Della.

"How about steppin' up and letting me paint you?"

There was enough innuendo in his tone to make Della blush. But of course it went right over the kids' heads. They only responded to the suggestion with laughs and encouragement for Della to let Yance paint her face.

"If you're going to do me, I'm going to do you," Della countered in a tone that unwittingly matched his, only increasing her own embarrassment.

And delighting him, if the grin that stretched his supple mouth was any indication.

His eyebrows rose, his blue eyes widened in mock anticipation and he said, "Can I take that as a promise?"

"Face painting, Culhane. Don't forget we're talking about face painting. If you paint my face, I'm painting yours," she clarified.

"Well, it's a start anyway. Come on over here." As he said that, his voice was so intimate that they could have been standing alone in a bedroom, with him beckoning her into his arms.

Or at least that's the image that sprouted in Della's mind and made sizzling little sparks dance along her nerve endings.

With the kids still urging her on, Della moved to stand in front of Yance, lifting her chin the way she might have for a kiss.

A kiss like the one he'd given her the night before...

She pushed that sweet morsel of memory—and the fact that it elicited even more of those sizzling little sparks—from her mind and said, "What are you going to do to me?"

She hadn't intended for that to come out sounding so hopeful or so seductive, either, but it had, making him smile that smile again. "Nothin' that'll hurt," he assured her with a wiggle to those eyebrows he'd raised before.

She could see him dip the brush in red paint and knew he was applying it to the crest of her left cheekbone, but she couldn't tell by the feel what work of art he was producing.

Not that she cared much. Not when standing as close to him as she was had awakened every sense to fill itself with him. With the scent of his aftershave; with the heat his big body exuded; with the sight of his ruggedly chiseled features and those incomparable blue eyes honed in on her face; with the deep, vibrant sound of his voice teasing her, teasing her kids, as he worked; with the unholy urge for her mouth to be pressed against his, tasting the nectar of kisses that could knock her socks off...

"There you go," he said when he'd finished.

It seemed as if he'd just begun. But then, she'd been so lost in him and what he could awaken inside her, that it might have been hours and hours for all she knew.

She put some effort into getting herself under control as he held up a hand mirror for her to see his masterpiece.

Two hearts entwined on her cheekbone.

"Hmm..." she muttered, curious as to what they signified. If they signified anything at all.

But Yance didn't explain one way or another. He merely said, "Like 'em?"

"You're an artist of rare talent," she teased.

He put the mirror back on the table and said, "Okay. Now you do me. But be gentle."

The innuendo was thick again, and his eyes glistened with mischief she was seeing in him more and more these days. It occurred to her that Yance had a much stronger streak of the devil in him than she'd ever realized.

Not that she didn't like it. Because she did.

It was just that it gave him a new dimension and it was strange to find that one existed in a man she thought she knew pretty well after all these years.

Strange and exciting. And it left her curious as to what other facets might exist in him that she had yet to discover.

But she camouflaged her curiosity by studying his face as if it were a canvas, hating the thought of altering it in any way but once more feeling those sizzling sparks at the thought of touching him.

"Don't make me look like a sissy now," he warned, joking.

As if anything she painted on that face could make him look like a sissy.

But thinking about what Billy would be wanting if he didn't have the ulterior motive of blending into brick walls, Della decided what she'd do.

She reached for the black paint and the red, too, and then wiggled her finger at him. "You're going to have to sit down or something for me to reach you."

He obliged, resting back on the edge of the table.

But his legs were long, and even bent at the knee they were quite a barrier. She tried reaching him from the side, but that was an awkward angle, plus he was still inches above her eye level.

"Maybe you should kneel down," she suggested.

He grinned. "Trying to get me on my knees to you, are you?"

"Unless you want me to paint your belly button." That had been a more intimate reference than she meant for it to be, but she didn't realize it until the words were out, embarrassing herself again. And amusing him.

But rather than rubbing it in, he bent over, clasped both his hands around her waist and pulled her to stand between thighs he spread wide to allow her access.

And Della didn't know which response to that was worse—the shock waves that rippled through her from where his hands stayed, bracketing her middle, or the blush that flooded her face full force over being in such a position with him, or the instant surge of desire so intense it nearly laid her low.

"Are you gonna do it, Mom?"

Doing "it" was exactly what Della was thinking about at that moment. But Ashley hadn't meant the same "it" that was on Della's mind.

She forced some control over herself, tried to put her thoughts back on the straight and narrow, tried to ignore the incredible feel of those big, work-toughened hands on her and—with unsteady hands of her own—began to paint a jagged, bloody scar along the right side of Yance's forehead and another diagonally across his right cheek.

The whole time she did, Yance stared down at her, not moving a muscle, focusing on her with a gaze as intense as a lover's caress. He seemed to be memorizing every pore, every line, every inch of her face. And liking what he saw, because the longer it went on, the more his lips eased into a private smile that seemed to reflect approval, appreciation, attraction....

Or maybe his thoughts were where hers had been when Ashley had yanked her out of them.

"Okay, you're done," Della announced when she couldn't bear any more of his scrutiny or the arousal he was stirring inside her.

She stepped back, out of his grasp, out from between his legs, and handed him the mirror so he could see her handiwork.

"Ooh, cool," Billy said while Yance was still surveying what she'd done.

"Pretty fair," he finally judged in a voice that seemed deeper, huskier and just a touch ragged around the edges, letting Della know she hadn't been the only one of them affected by whatever it was that had just gone on between them.

But then he seemed to regroup. He leaned over enough to say in hushed tones for her ears alone, ''I just hope this isn't a warning.''

''A warning?''

''That you're aimin' to leave me scarred.''

Did that mean that his painting on her face meant he intended to link his heart with hers?

''I'm not aiming for anything,'' she told him just as quietly. ''Are you?''

He only smiled a smile that left her guessing, without revealing anything at all.

Then he broke the intimacy that had somehow wrapped around them even in that crowded place and turned his attention to the kids.

Which was where it stayed for the next two hours as Yance concentrated on making the evening extra-special and fun for them.

Not even Bucky—who had been a good father—would have lasted as long or been as tireless as Yance was. He made sure each child got to do every game, negotiated compromises when not all of them were agreeable to what order the games would follow, and even took the kids outside and around the school building so they could go through the haunted house a second and a third time when they asked him to.

Not that he ignored Della along the way, because he didn't. He made sure he had her permission for everything, he teased her, joked with her, threw her wicked winks over the kids' heads and every now and then leaned in to whisper something in her ear. Nothing of any particular importance, but the feel of his warm breath against her skin was still enough to make her go light-headed each time he did it.

He was also so in tune with the kids and their needs that he noticed they were winding down before it even occurred to Della.

Or maybe it would have, except that she was having such trouble keeping her thoughts from wandering to Yance, from watching him, from being pleased by all she saw and enjoying herself...and him...so much.

But it was well after all the kids' bedtimes, and so of course they were dragging. In fact, Nic seemed to have taken up permanent residence on Yance's back, with his legs wrapped round Yance's middle, his arms around his neck and his head on Yance's shoulder.

But rather than suggesting they call it a night, Yance said, "How 'bout we have a cup of that homemade apple cider and sit awhile in the cafeteria?"

Della didn't want the night to end, didn't want to say goodbye to him and leave him behind. But she had her kids to think of and so she said, "Sounds good, but I should probably get everybody home."

"I want some slider," Billy piped up.

"Cider," Della corrected. "And how can you want some if you can't even say it?"

"I want some and I can say it—slider," Nic said, making them all laugh and proving that both her boys were as reluctant as she was to call quits to the impromptu evening with Yance even though they were beat.

"Just one cup," Yance cajoled.

"Yeah, just one cup," both her girls chimed in at once, and so Della let the majority rule.

The kids were all a little punchy and a lot silly by then and kept up a giggling patter through the cider. That was when Della really knew it was time to get them home.

Once she'd made that clear to everyone, Yance said, "How 'bout I follow you, then? Make sure you get there all right."

"It's only ten blocks," Della reminded him much the way he'd pointed it out to her the day he'd brought Billy home and she'd been fretting about the snowstorm.

"But ghosts and goblins are out on nights like these," he warned. "And I have magic powers to fight them off."

He had magic powers, all right. But they all worked on Della.

Still, the boys overheard enough to start begging for a ride in his truck, and without too much of a struggle, Della gave in to that, too. Again with more thought to prolonging their time together than anything else.

It was a fast trip to her house, and as Della and the girls climbed the steps onto the porch, Yance followed the boys up the walk from where he'd parked at the curb.

Della dispatched the kids upstairs to wash faces, get into pajamas and go to bed to wait for her to tuck them all in. Then she turned to Yance where he stood just inside the still open front door.

"Would you like a cup of coffee?" she asked, wishing she hadn't sounded so hopeful.

"I think I better pass. Let you get some rest." But he didn't move from that spot. "Did you mind too much that I horned in on you guys tonight?"

"No!" Too quick and emphatic. She amended her tone as her natural bluntness kicked in and she couldn't help adding, "But I'm still sort of confused about why you did. About what's going on with you." *And me*, she almost said, stopping herself at the last minute because that seemed to assume more than she thought she should.

Yance smiled a slow smile that crinkled the corners of his eyes. "You mean you don't know by now?"

"I guess not. I mean, hanging out at the school's haunted house isn't a real exciting way to spend an evening."

"I told you, that depends on who you're spendin' it with. Are you havin' some trouble believing that I might just want to be with you, Del?"

Okay, so she wasn't the only one who could be blunt.

He reached out one hand then, clasping it around her upper arm to pull her to stand close in front of him, much the way she had when she'd painted his face except his legs weren't on either side of her. Unfortunately...

"It probably sounds strange since we've known each other our whole lives and never been much more than passin' acquaintances, but I'm findin' myself just a little bit crazy about you, Delaware."

"Just a little?" she countered, making a joke because she didn't know what to say to that, either.

But he didn't address the joke. Instead, he said,

"From the minute I heard you say where you'd be this evening, all I could think about was being there, too. Being with you and the kids. That's why I went. That's the only reason I went. But if you wish I hadn't, then just say the word and it'll never happen again."

Della shook her head, feeling as if she were going out on a very shaky limb. But still she said, "I don't wish you would have stayed home tonight. I didn't from the moment I saw you. I was glad you were there." Then she realized she was further out on that limb than she could be comfortable with and added, "You made it a great time for the kids. They wouldn't have had half as much fun without you."

A tiny frown creased a line between his brows. "Good," he said in contradiction to that expression. "But what about you?"

"I had a great time, too."

That sounded glib and generic, and she knew it wasn't what he wanted to hear.

He let silence hang there between them as he searched her face, delved into her eyes.

But apparently he didn't see enough to satisfy him because he said, "Would you rather I just pay attention to the kids and leave you alone?"

So he wasn't going to let her retreat from that limb after all. Or at least if she did, she knew that would be the end for her with Yance. That it would keep him from ever again paying her the slightest heed as anything other than the mother of Ashley, April, Billy and Nic.

And the mere idea of it rocked her. More than she thought it could have.

"No," she heard herself admit. "I wouldn't rather you only pay attention to the kids. I'm…" She couldn't make herself say she was a little bit crazy about him, too. Even though it was true. So instead, she said, "I'm liking…this. A lot."

The shadow of that frown disappeared, and she saw that streak of devilry reemerge in his blue eyes. "Are you likin' me just a little, too?"

She couldn't keep from smiling back at him; there was just something about his grin that was infectious. Something about this man himself that was infectious. "Yes, I'm liking you a little, too," she acknowledged.

"Any chance you could start liking me more than a little?"

"Well, anything's possible," she went on teasing him, surprised by the coquetry in her voice.

"So does that mean we're still havin' dinner tomorrow night?"

"I was planning on it."

"Hot damn," he whispered like an endearment, still smiling down at her.

His eyes were locked so firmly onto hers that she felt as if they were drawing her to him like magnets. But in reality it was his hands that were pulling her closer still.

When she got where he wanted her, he bent over. But he didn't kiss her the way she thought he was going to. He rubbed the tip of his nose against the tip of hers. Slowly, back and forth, as if testing to see if she was going to balk.

She didn't, though. How could she when she was hoping like mad that kissing was what he had in mind after all? When she was craving it so badly she could have cried?

He raised one index finger to her cheekbone, to the hearts he'd painted on the crest, outlining them in a feather stroke that reminded her they were there.

Then he slid his hand behind her head, tipped it back with only a hint of pressure to guide her, and finally...*finally*...covered her mouth with his.

Della's eyes drifted shut, she let her head fall even farther back into the cradle of his hand and, unlike the night before, she didn't just accept the kiss, didn't just let him work the wonders that had made his kisses notorious. She gave as good as she got. She met him, matched him. She parted her lips in answer to his and, when his tongue came courting, she met and matched that, too.

She even grew bold enough to raise her hands to his chest. To lay her palms flat against the rock-hard wall of his pectorals.

And when he wrapped his other arm around her, easing her nearer still, she not only went, not only allowed him to hold her tight against him, but she also let those palms slide up to his shoulders, let them snake around his neck to bring herself that much more firmly to him as their kiss deepened, as passion blossomed.

Mouths were open wide, hungrily seeking, savoring. Della felt that same sensation she had the previous night—as if Yance's whole body were enveloping hers, supporting hers, cherishing hers.

He tasted of the cider they'd just had—sweet and sour at once. His skin was smooth but rougher than hers, warm and just slightly leathery. But for all his toughness, his mouth was tender, even as his kiss was gently insistent, guiding her, leading her, showing her the way to new pleasures.

Della began to wonder things she knew she shouldn't be wondering. Like how it would feel to be doing this with him in the dark...

Lying down...

Without clothes keeping the feel of his bare skin from hers...

But just then, the sounds of her kids upstairs getting ready for bed penetrated her thoughts and she realized any one of them could come down at any minute.

And that cooled some of the ardor that was coursing through her at breakneck speed.

She ended the kiss, not easily or any too fast, but she ended it just the same, finding herself breathless even after Yance had given in to her silent message that that was enough.

But he still didn't let go of her completely. He just loosened his hold, let his hands drop to clasp them behind the small of her back, keeping her within the circle of his arms.

He smiled down at her again, a smile as intimate as if they'd just made love, before he bestowed the softest of kisses on the hearts on her cheekbone as if that somehow sealed the message he'd conveyed in painting them there.

Then he released her completely, and said, "Tomorrow night can't come soon enough for me."

Me, either, she thought, but couldn't bring herself to say.

Instead, she said, "Thanks for everything tonight.

For making it so much fun,'' she added in a hurry because the kiss was still so much on her mind she felt as if she were thanking him for that.

''Thanks for letting me butt in.''

''Anytime.''

That pleased him. She could tell by the sparkle that lit his blazing blue eyes.

Then he said good-night, pecked one more parting kiss on her lips and left.

Left her with the sense that she might actually be glowing with the warmth he'd spread all through her.

Left her with the feeling that all was right with the world.

A feeling she hadn't had in a year.

Was it possible that after Bucky's death, something good really was happening now? she asked herself.

She was a little afraid to think so.

But on the other hand, how could something—*someone*—who made her feel the way she felt at that moment be anything but good?

It couldn't be.

Yance couldn't be.

And yet she had experience with something that was very, very good taking a bad turn that was completely out of anyone's control, so she warned herself to keep a bit of reserve, not to pin too much on the way she felt right then, not to trust that it might go on forever.

But reserve or not, warning or not, she still couldn't help hoping that whatever seemed to be developing with Yance really was all it seemed to be.

Chapter Seven

Shoveling manure was nobody's favorite job on the Culhane ranch. Which was why Yance, Cully and Clint took turns. But for once Yance didn't mind it as he performed the chore the next day. In fact, he was in such a good mood he could have done just about anything and not minded.

The sun was out, high and bright in a clear autumn sky. The air was crisp and calm. And he'd just come off one evening with Della to look forward to another one tonight. So he was riding high.

He'd been a little skittish about showing up at the haunted house the previous evening. Uninvited. Unannounced. For all he knew, unwanted. Just appearing out of nowhere to hang around with Della and her kids.

But from the minute he'd overheard her tell her sister that was how she was spending Thursday night, he hadn't been able to think about anything but going, too. Standing in for Bucky with the kids to help make it special for them and maybe keep them from missing their father too much. Seeing Della...

By dusk the previous afternoon, he'd finally given in to the urge to act on those thoughts. He'd figured that if it looked as if he were inhibiting Della or any of her children by being there, or as if they'd have a better time without him, he'd make up an excuse and leave. But he just had to give it a try. Just in case.

And luckily none of the negatives had happened. Instead, it had seemed as if the Dennehys were enjoying his being there as much as he was enjoying being with them. So he'd stayed.

And been glad he did. Glad he'd gone in the first place.

He was thrilled that they'd welcomed him. That not only had the kids seemed to enjoy his company, but that Della had, too. Enough to let him talk her into lingering for cider when the kids were really ready to go home. Enough to let him con his way into seeing them to their front door. Enough to even invite him in for coffee as if she wasn't in too big a hurry to see him go—

"I'll be damned if you aren't the happiest lookin' manure shoveler I ever did see," Cully interrupted Yance's thoughts, coming into the barn where Yance had begun work on the stalls before moving out to the paddock.

Yance held a shovelful out to him. "Want some?"

Cully put up his hands, palms out to ward off even

the suggestion. "No, thanks. It's all yours. But how come you're having such a good time at it?"

"I'm not havin' a good time at this. I was just thinkin' about the good time I had last night. And the one I could be in line to have again tonight. I'm takin' Della out to dinner. Thought we might try that new place over in Carver City."

Cully whistled a long, steady stream of mock surprise and then goaded Yance, "You're takin' Della Dennehy out to dinner? Like on a date? All the way over to Carver? I thought you were just playing big brother to her kids. You playin' big brother to her now, too? Or is there more to it?"

Oh, there was more to it, all right. A lot more. But Yance wouldn't admit too much. "I'm not playin' big brother to her," was all he said.

"That's what I thought," Cully said as if it were about time Yance owned up to it. But then he turned more serious and added, "She ready for that?"

"For goin' out to eat dinner? I think so," Yance answered, even as the question rang a bell in him, reminding him of thoughts he'd had himself only a few days ago.

"That all there is to it? Just the two of you eatin' together?" Cully persisted.

This time it was Yance's brows that lifted in a shrug. "I only did the askin'. She did the acceptin'. You'd have to talk to her about whether or not there's more to it than just eatin'."

"That's not all there is to it for you, though. I haven't seen you this cheery since... Well, in three years."

"Since before Nancy and Jeremy died," Yance supplied for his brother. "What have I been? An old grump or somethin'?"

"No. But you didn't go around smiling through manure shoveling, either."

Yance just laughed at that. "I suppose I am feeling pretty perky, all right."

The sound of Ivey's voice drifted to them then, calling Cully from the house as if he were late for something.

"I'm on my way," he called back. But before he moved an inch, he said, "Be careful, boy. Della's a lot fresher than you are from losin' the love of her life. Could be she's not as ready to take up with another man yet and you could be headin' for heartache."

"Sounds like a song, 'Headed for Heartache,'" Yance joked.

"Just be careful, huh?" Cully said as he made his way out of the barn and left Yance to go back to his manure gathering.

But Cully's words stayed in Yance's mind.

Did he know any better now than he had before if Della was ready for a new relationship?

Or was he so caught up in her, in the way he felt when he was around her, the way he felt when he *wasn't* around her, in thinking of how to *be* around her, that he wasn't paying attention to whether she was ready or not? To whether or not he could be headed for heartache?

Not that he was sure where he was headed one way or another. But he was sure of one thing, he knew it involved his feelings. Which meant he'd better open his eyes and take a look at what might really be going on.

That wasn't difficult when it came to what was going on with him.

He liked Della more and more with each minute they spent together. More even than he had all those years ago when he'd had that schoolboy crush on her.

He admired the way she was coping with the loss of Bucky. He was impressed with her as a parent—she was kind and loving and compassionate, but firm enough to have well-behaved, well-mannered, nice kids. He enjoyed her sense of humor, especially when she took his teasing and shot back some of her own. He had a good time with her. He even liked her bluntness. There was no artifice to Della. No game playing. What he saw was what he got....

And oh, boy, did he like what he saw.

The woman could leave him hot and bothered with the simple turn of her head. She had eyes that literally twinkled when she smiled. A mouth that melted his insides every time it curved up at the corners. And then there was her body.

Small and tight but still soft. If he closed his eyes, he could feel it up against him again, the way it had been the night before. Feel those insistent little breasts pressed to his chest. Feel her hips up close to his...

Oh, yeah, he knew what was going on with him. He wanted her. He wanted her every which way. Enough to let him know this was no passing fancy on his part.

In fact, it occurred to him at that moment that he was fast coming to care for her in a way he'd only cared for one other woman in his life. The way he'd cared for Nancy.

But was Della ready for that?

What if she was just testing the waters of being single again and for her there wasn't anything deeper than that going on between them?

Yance paused with his shovel in midair as that thought struck him.

But if it was true, how did that kiss they'd ended the past evening with fit in?

It didn't.

That was *not* a testing-the-waters kiss. Not by a long shot, he told himself.

She'd let him hold her so close a hair couldn't have passed between them. She'd answered his kiss with one of her own. Openmouthed. Tongues playing.

She'd laid her hands on him as if she'd been as hungry to touch him as he'd been to touch her. She'd wrapped her arms around his neck and hung on, held him as tightly as he'd held her....

No, that had *not* been the kiss of someone who wasn't ready for it.

But being ready for a passionate kiss and being ready for a whole relationship could be two different things. So that still didn't tell him if she was ready for the same things he was ready for.

And that meant he could get hurt. That he really would be headed for heartache. Big time.

''Back off, then,'' he told himself out loud, his voice echoing in the empty barn.

But as soon as he'd said the words, he realized that he was already in too deep for that. He already had too many feelings invested not to try to take this as far as he could.

He'd just have to hope that he wasn't making a mistake. He had to hope that Della—being the sensible, down-to-earth woman she was—knew herself well enough to judge when she was ready for a new relationship. And that if she wasn't ready, no amount of cajoling or flirting or persuasion on his part would have been able to lure her into spending the time together that they'd already spent, or into agreeing to go out to dinner with him tonight. Or into kissing him the way she'd kissed him less than twenty-four hours ago.

"But it looks like I'm putting my heart in your hands," he said to the image of her in his mind, the image that stayed with him night and day now, the image that kept him stirred up, wanting to see her in person, wanting to be with her, just plain wanting her.

And the only thing he could do was trust her.

Trust her and trust his own instincts.

Because what his instincts were telling him every time he was with her, every time he looked into her beautiful bottle green eyes, every time he touched her, held her, kissed her, was that she wasn't doing any of this against her will or on a whim or just because she was testing the waters.

His instinct about her was that she was getting in as deep as he was.

Or maybe that was just what he was counting on.

Because to Yance, Della was beginning to look like the best thing that had happened to him since Nancy.

And he couldn't back off.

Headed for heartache or not.

* * *

The baby shower Della and Ivey gave for Savannah was at the Culhane ranch because that was where Ivey lived with Cully and it offered space enough to comfortably seat all the guests. And there were a lot of guests.

In a town the size of Elk Creek most of the women—whether they were particularly close to Savannah or not, whether they were young, old or in between—had to be invited or there would be hurt feelings.

Della and Ivey served finger sandwiches, vegetables and fruit with dips for each, potato and macaroni salads, and a sangria wine punch to kick things off.

Della didn't eat any of the food. It wasn't that she was saving room for her dinner out with Yance—it was just that she was too nervous to eat.

She did sip on the punch, though, hoping that might calm her nerves as it loosened everyone else's tongues and began the usual stories of childbirth experiences and a few admissions of couples trying to get pregnant. Those elicited encouragement and advice and some recipes for success for sex selection that were more comical than practical.

From there talk turned to the sex of Savannah's baby, which she and Clint had asked the doctors not to tell them even if it was obvious on the ultrasound tests that had been done to make sure things were progressing normally.

Someone suggested Savannah spit in drain cleaner to find out, which only brought laughs. Someone else had Savannah stand in the center of the room so they could judge by studying how she was carrying the baby, deciding it was a boy because she looked like she had a basketball stuffed under her smock and didn't even look pregnant from the back. And then Nanna Winter—who was nearly ninety-two—made Savannah lie on her back while Nanna held Savannah's wedding ring tied to the end of a string over the mound of her belly to see if it went around in a circle or back and forth. That verdict was that Savannah was going to have a girl.

After they'd cut and served the cake, everyone settled down to watch Savannah open her gifts, passing each one around so everyone could get a closer look.

The presents covered the gamut from teeny-tiny tennis shoes to clothes for a year-old baby, from diaper bags and a car seat to the crib and changing table that Ivey and Cully gave.

Everyone had been generous, and Della was glad to see her best friend so happy as she exclaimed over it all. Savannah and Clint deserved it, she thought, after their teenage romance had ended in a separation of over a decade before they'd finally been brought together again by Ivey's coming back to Elk Creek and connecting with Cully. It was high time Savannah and Clint had found each other again and were starting the family that might have begun so many years ago.

And yet something about the shower left Della feeling very melancholy.

Maybe it was the sangria on an empty stomach, she told herself.

But she didn't really believe it.

Because even as she watched her friend and kept a list of who gave what, and joked and oohed and aahed with the rest, she still felt somehow removed from it all.

But if it wasn't caused by the punch, then what was it caused by?

She didn't have an answer for that and so decided to stop drinking the sangria just in case.

But even without the punch, by the end of the shower Della still felt melancholy.

It made for a strange way to go out on her first date with anyone other than Bucky in twenty-four years.

"So what's up with you?" she asked her reflection in the mirror of one of the Culhanes' bathrooms when the last of the guests had gone, the mess had been cleared and she was freshening up to go to dinner with Yance.

But she still didn't have a ready answer for herself, and so, disturbed and uneasy, she brushed on a little more blush, reapplied lipstick, ran a comb through her bobbed hair and retucked her new, teal green silk blouse into the black slacks she'd worn for the occasion of both the shower and the date.

The date that maybe she shouldn't go on if she felt this way...

But even melancholia couldn't make her walk out of that bathroom and tell Yance she didn't want to go. She *did* want to go. She just didn't know what was wrong with her.

Yance was in the living room when she left the bathroom. The voices of Ivey, Savannah, Clint and Cully could be heard coming from the kitchen, but Yance was waiting for her alone. And looking as magnificent as always in black Western-cut pants that were a cross between jeans and slacks and a crisp white dress shirt with a stand-up collar banded in black at the base of his throat. He was clean shaved and smelled of that aftershave that made her head go light, and melancholy or not, Della couldn't imagine not going on that date with him.

Still and all, though, the melancholy colored her greeting and apparently her expression, too, because Yance's brows took a curtsy toward one another as if he knew something wasn't quite right with her.

"Hungry?" he guessed, as if that might be it.

"Mmm," was all she could muster. "Are you?"

"Starved. But I thought we'd take a drive over to Carver and try that new place. If you can last for a half hour ride."

She was glad they wouldn't be staying in town, glad to go to the nearby—and not so small—town of Carver to get away from the watchful eyes of Elk Creek. And she was grateful to Yance for suggesting it.

"That sounds good," she said, still more lackluster than she wanted to be.

Yance helped her on with the black blazer she'd bought for the occasion, shrugged into a short black leather jacket of his own, then opened both the front door and the truck door for her when they came to each of them.

And the whole time Della lectured herself to buck up, to shake off whatever it was that had a grip on her.

Yance had gone around the rear of his truck and when he got in on the driver's side, Della jumped as if she hadn't been expecting him. So this time his frown was full-blown as he started the engine and glanced over at her.

"You okay, Del?"

"I'm feeling a little funny, actually," she told him straight out.

"About the date? That's only natural, it being the first one."

"No, I don't think this is about the date. It started at the shower. When everybody was talking about how many kids Savannah and Clint want, and Ivey said she and Cully are expecting one of their own, and Ally and Jackson are trying, and Beth and Ash are ready for another baby even though Melissa is only a little over a year old, and—"

It suddenly dawned on Della what she was feeling.

"And?" Yance prompted as he drove past the last ranch that bordered Elk Creek and took them out into the open countryside that lay between there and Carver.

"And I started to think about how that part of my life is over and it made me feel sad. And old and sorry for myself," she finished with a laugh because, even though it was all true, it was nice to finally know where the melancholy was coming from.

Yance looked at her, poking his chin out and studying her. "I'm not seein' any gray hairs. Or wrinkles, either. You don't look all that old to me."

"Only because you're a year older," she joked.

"And a year wiser," he said smugly.

"Ah. And what does your greater wisdom tell you about this?"

"That you're crazy."

Della laughed again. "Oh, thanks. I'm not old but I am crazy."

"You're crazy if you think you're over the hill," he qualified.

"Well, maybe not over the hill, exactly. Just past what everybody else seems to be doing. And jealous that they're doing it and I'm not, I guess."

"Jealous of people havin' babies?"

"Okay, okay, I know it does sound crazy when I've already had four of my own. But—"

"Doesn't sound crazy to me. Not if you want more." He shot her a sidelong glance. "Do you want more?" he asked as if he had a keen interest in the answer and wasn't only making conversation.

"I'm not sure," she admitted, laughing yet again at herself, but thinking about that for the first time just the same. "Before today, I'd have said no. Four kids is a houseful. Not to mention a handful."

"But now?"

Della considered that. "But now I'm feeling a lot differently than I have in the past. About everything. About myself. About life in general. Maybe about starting over again and even having more babies."

Yance grinned at her. "Sounds good to me," he said as if she'd been inviting him to father them. Then he changed his tone to one that was less teasing. "Congratulations."

"For what?"

"You're on the road."

"The road to Carver?" she said with a nod to the town that was just coming into view.

"The road back to the land of the living. You've

just realized that even though you've lost the person you loved more than you loved to breathe, you're still alive. And you want to be—that's the most important part. You *want* to go on living. Even without Bucky. That's a big step.''

And a different perspective from which to look at this. ''So you're saying that instead of thinking that the baby part of my life is over and feeling sad about it, I should realize that it doesn't have to be over at all? That it's over for me with Bucky, but that that doesn't mean I can't have more kids with someone else if I want them? That it doesn't mean I can't have anything else I want, too?''

''That's what I'm sayin'.'' He did a slight side bend toward her and confided, ''There isn't anything that *has* to be over for you if you don't want it to be, Del.''

''Chocolate-chip ice cream,'' she said out of the blue, remembering his telling her he hadn't been able to eat it after his wife's death.

''Chocolate-chip ice cream,'' he confirmed. ''First you go through guilt that you're still around to enjoy it. Then you accept that you are still around to enjoy it. And then you do.''

''Eat it on a regular basis now, do you?'' And that sounded as if she were referring to more than a bowl of ice cream.

Yance smiled at her again. ''A lot of nights I have a dish, yes, ma'am.''

''And it tastes as good?''

He gave her a very soft smile then. ''Yeah, it does. Just as good. And I love it just as much.''

They'd arrived at the restaurant that sat in the center

of Carver. It was an old, two-story frame house that was loftily titled Villa Napoli.

But if the smells of garlic and herbs coming from the place were a clue to the quality of the food, it might not be too lofty a name after all.

Yance found a parking spot, pulled in and turned off the engine.

"Thanks," Della said before he could get out.

"For what? I haven't fed you yet."

"For walking me through this stuff."

He winked at her. "My pleasure. Feel better?"

"Much," she said honestly. In fact, the melancholia was gone completely, she was enjoying herself—and him—and she felt rejuvenated, and it was all thanks to this man sitting only a few feet away, looking so handsome it nearly made her heart melt.

It left her with an inordinate urge for him to kiss her for some reason she didn't understand. Right there. Right then.

But he didn't do it because of course he couldn't know what was going through her mind at the moment.

So she did it.

She leaned toward him and pressed a quick kiss to his lips. Nothing passionate or long and drawn out, just a brief meeting of her lips to his, shocking them both, hardly fulfilling the real craving she had, but pleasing Yance—who grinned at her as if he were a kid on Christmas morning.

"Don't get me wrong—I'm not complaining—but what was that for?"

"Just because I wanted to," she said, feeling bold.

"Anything else you want to do?" he asked with a devilish wiggle to his eyebrows.

"Eat dinner," she said, happy to tease him.

Yance just laughed, got out of the truck and came around for her.

But that kiss seemed to set them on a different course than they'd been on before. When he opened the truck door for her, he reached in and took her hand to help her out, keeping hold of it all the way into the restaurant, all the way to their table.

Not that Della regretted it, because she didn't. In fact, her hand seemed to fit into his as if it had been carved from the same stone. The nail-buffer texture of his calluses felt good against her softer palm, and the warmth and power of his touch sluiced in through her pores and ran like hot lava all the way up her arm.

He sat just around the corner from her rather than across the table and didn't hesitate to take her hand again—often—as they ate salads laden with mozzarella cheese, pepperoni, black olives and vinaigrette dressing, or as they dipped rosemary-topped focaccia bread into spiced olive oil.

Yance even tasted her lasagna and fed her some of his rigatoni as their dinner progressed and any inhibitions they'd had with one another seemed to have been left somewhere out on the country road they'd traveled to get there.

By the time they headed for home, Della felt so comfortable with Yance, so close to him, so renewed, she almost slid across the truck's bench seat to sit right beside him as he drove.

Almost. But not quite.

Instead, she angled herself his way so she could drink in the sight of his perfect profile.

And it *was* perfect. Rugged, masculine, gorgeously handsome. Just looking at him set off a tingling sensation in the pit of her stomach and made her wonder how anyone as terrific looking as he was, as nice as he was, hadn't been snatched up by some single woman.

"So, if you're past the grief and the guilt, and have moved on to enjoying chocolate-chip ice cream again, why haven't you remarried and started over after all this time?" she asked as they hit the open road once more.

He shrugged a shoulder and when he did she remembered too vividly having run a hand across it the night before, remembered how solid it was. How powerful. How good it had felt...

"I just haven't found anyone I wanted to start over with."

Until now...

Did those words hang in the air even though he hadn't spoken them?

It seemed to Della that they did. But she couldn't be sure. Maybe she was just imagining it. Maybe it was just wishful thinking....

"What about you, Del? Think you're ready for a new relationship?"

That took her by surprise. Especially since he asked it very solemnly, as if it was particularly important to him.

"I don't know," she answered truthfully, thinking about it. Then she said, "I guess having dinner with you tonight, seeing you as much as I have been, is sort of a new relationship, isn't it?''

He looked at her, his eyes penetrating the dimness of the truck cab with their intensity. ''It feels that way to me. Has that been okay?''

Again she considered it, trying it on for size.

''Yeah,'' she decided. ''It's been more than okay. It's been nice. Really nice.''

He grinned as if she'd said just the right thing and couldn't have pleased him more. ''Does that mean if I did what I've been wanting to do since we pulled into that restaurant's parking lot you wouldn't mind too much?''

''I guess that depends on what it is you want to do.''

Without saying any more, he turned onto the next dirt road they came to, went a short distance away from the main highway and came to a stop at a spot where fallow cornfields and a clear night sky full of stars were what they were looking out upon.

Then he turned off the engine, draped one thick wrist over the steering wheel and stretched his other arm along the seat back, letting his gaze settle on her.

''What you've wanted to do is park the truck and stare at me?'' she asked, joking.

He eased himself to the middle of the seat, reached for her, pulled her to meet him there and gave her a kiss that made hers from earlier pale into nothingness by comparison. A kiss that was adept and masterful and so mind-bogglingly incredible that in the few moments that it lasted, it managed to make every nerve ending in her body rise to the surface of her skin. It made her head go much lighter than even his aftershave had, made her muscles turn to jelly, her toes curl and her nipples harden into tight kernels.

And when he stopped kissing her, opening her eyes and coming back to earth were delayed responses she had some trouble accomplishing at all.

"Now, *that* was a kiss," he said with a wicked grin. "Don't you ever again give me one of those 'thanks, brother' things like you did when we got to the restaurant."

Then he slid back behind the wheel, taking her with him to sit where she'd wanted to sit before—close beside him.

"You know," she said, looking at him as he started the engine again, turned the truck around and retraced their path back to the main road, "I always thought of you as the quiet, shy Culhane brother."

He laughed at that, shot her an arched-eyebrow glance and said, "Think better of it, Delaware."

She did think better of it the whole rest of the drive home, even as they chatted about inconsequential things. She thought about that and all the ways in which he was surprising her. And she thought about that kiss he'd just given her and how her blood was still running hot from it. She thought about how thick and hard muscled his thighs were running the length of hers. And how his hands looked on the steering wheel—big and capable, controlling it with an easy, experienced touch that she kept imagining on her skin, instead.

She also thought about the way his biceps brushed her shoulder. And how much she liked his citrusy scent. And the sharpness of his jawline. And the fact that he had the longest eyelashes she'd ever seen on a man.

And how, if he turned down the invitation she was going to extend for coffee and left her too early tonight, she just might scream....

But he didn't turn her down.

When they arrived back at her place and she asked him in, He accepted without hesitation. He even offered to make the coffee as she said good-night to the baby-sitter, who could walk home since she lived just next door.

Della could hear him clattering around her kitchen as she went upstairs to check on the kids, discovering all four of them sound asleep. She tucked in blankets and pried Billy's stuffed rabbit out from under him, leaving no one's door open more than a crack when she was finished.

Then she returned downstairs, finding Yance waiting for her in the living room with two steaming cups of coffee on the coffee table—side by side—in front of where he was sitting in the center of the sofa with one arm stretched enticingly along the back.

He patted the cushion right next to him suggestively, and Della couldn't resist taking him up on that suggestion.

She sat there, sharing that middle ground, almost as near to him as he'd placed her himself on the truck seat.

"You know," he said, mimicking her beginning when she'd commented earlier about always having thought of him as being quiet and shy, "I had one hell of a crush on you in the eighth grade."

"No, you didn't," she answered, sure he was teasing her again.

"Oh, yes, I did. I had a secret notebook with every one of your class pictures in it from kindergarten on. I followed you home from school for all of two weeks and I did a lot of that calling-and-hanging-up stuff, hoping to hear your voice but never having the guts to ask to speak to you or to talk if you did answer."

"Then you *were* shy."

"About you I was. Then, anyway." His smile was warm and soft as he looked into her eyes with those blazing blue ones of his, and laid his palm tenderly to the side of her face. "I just couldn't get up the courage to let you know what was goin' on with me."

"And then Bucky moved to town—"

"And that took care of that."

"I hope you didn't have hurt feelings."

"It was like a stab through the heart," he confided in a tone that sounded much too sexy to truly convey that. "I got over it, though. Well, I got over the stab through the heart. Maybe I never did get over the crush...."

There was something almost hypnotic in his voice, in the way he was still caressing her face, in the hold his eyes had over hers. Della could only smile up at him and feel once more all the sensations his kiss on the open road had awakened in her.

And then he kissed her again. More slowly this time. More leisurely. More sweetly.

For a while, at least.

Then the arm that was across the back of the couch came around her. The hand that had been stroking her face slipped to the back of her head to cradle it against a kiss that grew rapidly intense. Yance's lips parted over hers. And Della responded in kind, welcoming his tongue when it came calling, circling it, playing all the games he initiated and initiating a few of her own.

Her arms were around him even though she didn't remember putting them there, and her already hardened nipples nuzzled against his chest, feeling confined, constrained, craving that same caress he'd given her face until moments before.

Maybe her back arched, calling a little more attention there. Or maybe he really could read her mind after all, because the hand that was cupping the back of her head started a slow, tantalizing descent. To the side of her neck, where featherlight circles ignited flames inside her. To her shoulder, where he did some of the kneading her breasts were crying out for. And down farther still until that hand finally covered one yearning orb.

Lord, how was it possible for a woman her age, the mother of four children, to feel as if that were the first time a man had ever put a hand on her breast? But that was how it seemed to her. Exciting, thrilling, new and wonderful.

But, oh, it just wasn't enough!

The silk of her blouse was light. The sheer lace of her bra wasn't too much heavier, and yet they could have been armor for the barrier they made between that magical hand and the throbbing need of her bare breast.

This time she knew very well that her back arched more, arched so that she thrust her breast firmly into his grasp, because she did it on purpose.

And Yance answered it as if it were as clear to him as the written word. But he answered not only with the unbuttoning of her blouse, with the easing down of her bra cup, but with a kiss that deepened even more at the same time. With a mouth that opened wide and hungrily. With a tongue that stopped playing and turned more insistent, more passionate.

And then his hand—warm and work toughened—finally found the ultrasensitive bare breast that was engorged with wanting just that.

Had anything ever felt that good?

If it had, she didn't remember. And it flashed through her mind that Yance Culhane had not only deserved a glowing reputation for his kisses, but also for the wonders of his touch.

He traced her nipple with loving care, circled it, brushing across the crest again and again until it hardened in such delight it almost hurt. Almost. But not quite. Or at least not with any kind of pain that she didn't want to go on and on.

And then his mouth left hers to rain hot, moist kisses down the hollow of her throat, all the way to the center of her breastbone.

Delicious torture—that's what it was as he kissed a slow path to where his hand kneaded, squeezed and finally lifted her into the warm recesses of that gifted mouth.

Della's head fell back, her breath caught in her throat and her spine arched even more as his tongue flicked the straining glory of her nipple, as he drew her flesh deeply into that velvet darkness.

More. She wanted more, she thought as she pressed

her palms to his hard, bulging biceps. As they seemed to slide on their own volition to the sides of his waist, to the sides of his hips…

But that was when Yance put an end to it all.

Not easily, if the groan of misery that accompanied it was any indication. But end it he did nevertheless, rising up from her breast, taking her hands in both of his to remove them before she could get further than she had and bringing them to his mouth, where he buried kisses in her palms.

"Any more and I'm not gonna be able to control myself."

"Good," she heard herself whisper, surprised at her own imprudence.

But Yance shook his head in denial. "I want you to think about this before we do it," he said, giving that advice for the second time tonight, in a voice that was husky and passion ragged. "I don't want to rush you. I don't want you to rush into it. I sure as hell don't want it to be something you regret afterward."

It would have taken a fire hose full of cold water to cool her off at that moment, and this was just a finger splash. But still Della fought the wild yearnings inside her and tried to grasp what he was saying.

He kissed her again—short, quick, urgently—and then stood.

"Think it over, Della," he said. "Think it over long and hard. Because when—if—we do this, there won't be any turnin' back. Not for me. So you need to be real, real sure."

And then he left.

Della was too love stung to walk him out. To even

move. She just sat where he'd left her, her breasts still heaving from within the open buttons of her blouse. Her body still craving a completion of what he'd begun. Still craving him with a hunger she'd believed she'd never feel again.

But what she was thinking about wasn't whether or not she was ready for a new relationship. She wasn't thinking about her own misconception of Yance as the shy, quiet Culhane brother. She wasn't even thinking about whether or not she really had wanted him to make love to her.

She was thinking that if he had, she couldn't imagine herself regretting it afterward.

Chapter Eight

The alarm was set for six forty-five the next morning, but when one of her kids crawled into Della's bed at six, she didn't need to see the face to know who it was. Seven-year-old April was the earliest riser in the house, and most mornings her mother's bed was where she came first.

"Why are you up so early, April?" Della asked in a monotone, her eyes still closed.

"'Cause I waked up," the little girl answered. "Isn't it time yet?"

"You know it isn't."

"I'll jus' lay here and be quiet and you can sleep some more."

Della didn't respond to that. She merely rolled onto her back and waited.

Not two minutes later her daughter said, "Did you have a nice dinner with Yance last night?"

Della smiled sleepily. "Mm-hmm. Did you guys do all right with Heather?"

"Yep. She didn't even talk on the telephone too much before we went to sleep and she let us eat gra'm crackers and stay up a whole half hour late."

"Mmm."

"Did you go to the café and have the special candles like Ashley did when she goed to dinner with Yance?"

"When she *went* to dinner with Yance," Della corrected. Then she said, "No, we went to a new place in Carver. But there were candles on the tables."

"I like candles."

"Mmm."

"Ashley got to go out to dinner with Yance and have candles, and now you got to, too. When do me and Nic and Billy get to?"

Ah, the logic of children. And how was she supposed to answer that? Della thought.

"Ashley got to go for her birthday, and my dinner with Yance was a grown-up dinner."

"So when it's my birthday, will I get to go to dinner with Yance and have candles?"

Good question. Would he be true to his word and keep on being a big brother to the kids long enough for each of them to have a turn at a one-on-one birthday dinner with him?

"I don't know," she said to both her daughter's query and her own musings. "We'll see."

"Is Yance gonna come and live with us?"

Nice thought...

And it surprised Della that it was.

She counteracted her wandering imagination with a firm, "No, Yance is not going to come and live with us. He's just a friend. A good friend."

"Mary Alice's mommy's good friend moved in with them after her daddy went away."

"I know." The whole town knew. And had gossiped about it to no end.

"But I'm not sure if I'd like that or not," April added.

Della didn't understand why, but her heart sank a little at that simple statement. "Don't you like Yance?"

"Yes, I do. I like him lots. But Mary Alice's daddy lived with them and then he went away and Mary Alice was sad, and then her mommy's good friend Tom moved in and then he went away, too, and Mary Alice was sad again. Our daddy went away and I was sad, and if Yance comes to live with us maybe he might go away then, too, and I'd have to be sad again."

Della opened her eyes and looked over at her daughter's precious face where she lay on the pillow next to hers. Then she stretched an arm under April's head and pulled her to lie close to her side.

"Mary Alice's daddy went away because he *wanted* to. Your daddy didn't want to leave you. He was taken away from us by a heart attack."

"But maybe if Yance came to live with us he'd have a heart attack and die, too. Or maybe he'd just go away like Mary Alice's Tom did."

Something inside Della knotted up tight at that

thought. But she ignored it and concentrated on her daughter.

"I only went to dinner with Yance, April. I don't think we have to worry about him moving in or dying or any of this stuff, do you?"

"I just don't want to be sad that way again. Not ever."

"I don't want to be sad that way again, either," Della said, slightly taken aback by the unexpectedly deep conviction that came out in her voice. "But for now I think we can just enjoy having Yance as our friend, don't you?"

April nodded her agreement vigorously. Then she confided in a girlish whisper, "Me and Ash think he's cute. Ash likes his big muscles, but I think he has pretty eyes."

Ah, well. At least now she knew her daughters had taste.

"Do you think he's cute?" April asked.

"I think he's a very nice-looking man," Della said, sounding formal and stilted. But she could hardly admit to her daughter that she found Yance so handsome, so smolderingly sexy that sometimes she couldn't see straight.

"He's a babe," April said with a giggle.

Della glanced down at her. "Where did you get a word like that?"

"Mary Alice said her mommy said it about Yance when she saw him with us at the haunted house. Mary Alice said her mommy wanted to snatch him up— whatever that means."

It meant that Mary Alice's mother was living up to

her less-than-glowing reputation. But Della didn't say that.

It also meant that a wave of jealousy washed through Della. Along with an inordinate urge to tell April to tell Mary Alice to tell her mother to keep her distance from Yance.

But she didn't say that, either.

"Could Yance come trick-or-treating with us tonight?" April asked then.

"Do you want him to?" Della responded in amazement. Every year the kids complained about having a parent along at all. It cramped their style when they wanted to be out gathering candy incognito, and they were convinced that the only thing that gave them away was having either Della or Bucky waiting at the curb.

"Yance was lots of fun at the haunted house," April said. "I think he'd be fun trick-or-treating, too. Can we ask him to come?"

"I don't know. I'll have to think about it," Della said, remembering all too vividly how the previous night had ended and what she'd been assigned to think about because of it—what she hadn't been able *not* to think about since then.

Given that, she couldn't help wondering what message might be conveyed if she called Yance today and invited him over. He might take it at face value, figure he'd been a hit with the kids, that he'd earned their desire to have him included in the Halloween festivities and there was nothing more to it.

Or he might take it to mean she'd considered making love with him the way she very nearly had last night and had decided that she wanted to go through with it after all.

Did she mind if that second message was what he took from a trick-or-treating invitation?

If she was honest with herself, she realized that she didn't mind. That, in fact, inviting him to go trick-or-treating was a tailor-made excuse to get to see him again.

And if things should take more of that natural course they'd taken the night before?

Della's heart pounded with too much excitement to pretend she'd be sorry.

The alarm went off just then, jolting her out of her thoughts and causing April to bounce up as if it had been a shot from a starting gun.

"Happy Halloween!" the little girl shouted.

"Happy Halloween," Della answered with a laugh, wondering if she really should call Yance to join them tonight.

And just how happy a Halloween that might make it for her...

In Della's nine years of motherhood one of the things she'd learned was that children loved Halloween every bit as much as—if not more than—they loved Christmas. That made for four very unruly kids that morning as she tried to get them ready for a special Saturday session of Sunday school. The church was holding it today so that afterward the kids could be treated to a party and parade to show off their costumes.

Della's brood all wanted to wear their costumes at

the outset and had to be firmly told that they couldn't, that the costumes had to be packed and brought with them to be put on later, but that regular school clothes had to be what they wore until party time.

No one wanted oatmeal, toast, eggs or juice for breakfast. They wanted cold cereal. But Della put her foot down about it, refusing to let them start out what would be a sugar-soaked day with a sweet breakfast to boot.

She got them out the door barely five minutes before their classes started and into the car complete with coats, hats, mittens and all the parts that made up their costumes. But once she'd accomplished dropping them off at the church, it was wonderful to come back to a quiet house.

She hadn't had breakfast herself yet, but it wasn't food that was on her mind. There was something else she wanted to do. Before she lost her nerve.

She went straight to the telephone and called Yance.

It had been unanimous—all four kids wanted him along trick-or-treating—so she told herself that was the sole reason she was extending the invitation and dialed his number.

His machine answered, no doubt because he was already out working somewhere on the ranch by then. She left a brief message saying only that by request of Ashley, April, Billy and Nic, he was cordially invited to go trick-or-treating tonight. But only if he really wanted to...

Which left her fighting visions of what *she* really wanted to do with him tonight. And trick-or-treating had nothing to do with it.

Della was free until noon. She put the house in order, and then, with time on her hands, decided to give herself a beauty day.

Not with Yance or anything in particular in mind, she told herself. Just as a Halloween treat of her own.

She shaved her legs and under her arms with special care, put a mud mask on her face, did a hot-oil treatment on her hair and soaked for nearly an hour in a steamy bubble bath.

Then, as her hair air dried, she painted her toenails a bright pink color, put a clear polish on her fingernails and sat with cucumber slices on her eyes. Not that she knew why she was sitting with cucumber slices on her eyes, but she'd seen it in movies and she had a cucumber in the fridge, so she thought, Why not?

Dressing was a little more complicated, and as she stood in front of her closet she couldn't deny that Yance and the possibility of seeing him tonight were an influence. She wanted to wear something that would take his breath away.

But among the new things she'd purchased when she and Kansas had revamped her wardrobe with smaller sizes, the few choices that would accomplish that were inappropriate for walking the streets trick-or-treating later on.

She finally decided on a black knit jumpsuit with a zipper up the front from her waist to the high collar that wrapped her neck. The color, she reasoned, was not only right for Halloween, but sophisticated, too. And the fact that it hugged her smoother curves with a subtle slinkiness was just an added bonus. Plus, it was wrinkle proof—a benefit since she would have it on most all afternoon and into the evening because she'd be too busy to change.

The Halloween parade through the church basement and around the grounds was always hilarious. Kids and teachers—all in costume—lined up to preen in character along the way.

Afterward there was a big party complete with a hot lunch, cupcakes, ice cream and fruit punch. Awards were given for the best two costumes in each age group, and the minister held everyone's rapt attention by reading a book that was just spooky enough to keep the kids on the edges of their seats without really frightening anyone.

The party lasted the whole afternoon and by the time Della got the kids home, there was a message on her answering machine from Yance, saying he'd definitely be over for trick-or-treating that night.

That's all he said. He sounded happy and enthusiastic but he didn't say anything that would lead Della to believe the conclusion of the previous evening was on his mind at all. Certainly not the way it was on her mind.

But still, just hearing his deep, rich voice on the tape was enough to send goose bumps up her arms.

She and the kids carved two pumpkins, buried stubby candles within their hollowed insides and set them out on the porch railing. Then they fixed a quick supper of homemade pizza that the kids were mostly too excited to eat. But then, so was Della, if the truth be known.

With all that out of the way, the four kids and Della,

too, stood at the big picture window in the living room watching for darkness to descend and Yance to arrive.

Both things happened almost at the same time, with Yance's white truck slicing through the dim haze of dusk to park at the curb in front of the house.

It was cause enough for the kids to let off some pent-up excitement, running around, hooting and hollering like banshees.

Della, of course, couldn't jump for joy or hoot or holler, but she felt the same exuberance her children did. Only she wasn't on a sugar-induced high the way they were. For her, glee came in a tall, long-legged package dressed in cowboy boots, snug black jeans, a bright red shirt, a sheepskin coat and a Stetson pulled low over his brow.

The kids beat her to the door to let Yance in, but as he came across the threshold, removing his hat in one swipe and stepping into the circle of kids who did a dance around him as if he were a maypole, he had eyes only for Della.

"Hi, there," he said so softly it was barely audible over the kids' voices begging to go out trick-or-treating right that instant.

"Hi," she said back, feasting on the sight of him.

His gorgeous, blazing blue eyes went from her just combed hair to her freshened makeup, down the length of the jumpsuit and up again, hardly hesitating over too many spots but still giving her the sense that he was caressing her with that glance.

"Plee-eeze can't we go trick-or-treating now?" Billy broke in with a louder voice than the rest.

Yance shot Della a smile that said *later,* and turned his attention downward toward her kids.

"Who do we have here?" he asked as if he didn't recognize them.

"I'm Pocahontas," Ashley offered.

"I'm a bronc buster," Billy announced.

"I'm Belle from *Beauty and The Beast,*" April put in.

And Nic planted his feet apart, put his hands on his hips, lowered his voice comically and said, "I'm Megatron, man of steel."

Yance laughed, put his Stetson on Billy's head, and said, "You all look great."

"Where's your monster mask?" Billy demanded.

"You know, I was gonna bring it, but at the last minute I forgot the danged thing," Yance said, winking at Della. "Looks like I'll just have to scare folks with my regular face."

As if that were possible, Della thought, struck anew by just how handsome that chiseled face was and thinking that there was no doubt he was a babe—as April had called him that morning.

"Can we go now?" April asked, adding, "It's dark out and Yance is here."

"Yes, we can go now," Della said in exasperation.

"Wait, not yet. First, where are your bags?" Yance asked.

Eight tiny feet scrambled to retrieve from the living room the pillowcases they were going to use. When they'd sorted through whose was whose, the Dennehy brood brought them back to the entryway as quick as they could, holding the cases out in front of them like gaping mouths.

From inside his coat Yance took four lumpy orange plastic bags with black pumpkins on them. It was obvious they were crammed with goodies as he dropped them in each of the waiting pillowcases.

"Okay, that'll get you started. Now, let's go," he said, sounding like a coach sending his team out onto the field.

And so began two hours of trick-or-treating, running from door to door, hiding behind bushes to jump out at friends the kids caught sight of before the friends caught sight of them, innocent pranks that Yance instigated and an all-around Halloween Della knew her kids would never forget.

By design the last stop was Kansas and Linc's house. Kansas was having a sleepover for her stepson Danny and Della's four kids. Della had already given Kansas a suitcase full of spending-the-night necessities when they'd both been at the church earlier for the parade and party, and now all Della needed to do was drop off the kids.

Everyone filed in without too much complaint that the candy-gathering portion of the night was at an end because by then the cold temperatures had seeped in even under coats and costumes.

Kansas had hot cider waiting to warm them up, and while they drank it, Della went through all the pillowcases to make sure the kids' treats were safe. As she did, the kids, Yance and Linc answered the door to more trick-or-treaters, being ornery and making them all perform tricks for their treats rather than merely handing out candy.

By nine o'clock, when the doorbell had stopped ringing and Linc was bribing the children with the scariest ghost story they'd ever heard if they got ready for bed, Della finally decided she and Yance could be on their way.

On their way to where—or to what—she wasn't sure, but on their way, nevertheless.

They said good-night, Della kissed each of her kids and told them to behave and she and Yance bundled back up and went out into the cold October air once again.

"Well, there you have it—Halloween. I hope it was everything you expected when you said you'd come tonight," Della said just to get conversation started between them as they headed in the direction of her house. They'd both focused on the kids so much tonight that they'd hardly exchanged ten sentences with each other, and she didn't know where else to begin now that they were alone.

"I had a ball," he assured her convincingly. Then he added with a sly note to his voice, "I should have thanked the kids for inviting me."

"It *was* their idea," she said. "April suggested it early this morning, and everybody chimed in on the subject at breakfast when I asked them how they felt about it."

"How did you feel about it?"

"I was surprised. They usually don't want any adults along."

"How'd you feel about my comin'?" he specified

when she'd purposely taken the wrong meaning to his first question.

Della shot him a sideways glance. "Are you fishing for a compliment?"

He looked over at her and raised just one eyebrow. "I'm fishin' to know whether you wanted me with you tonight or not."

"I was glad you were coming," she said with a note of teasing to her voice that made it sound airy and none too serious.

"Glad enough to spend a little more time with me tonight? On our own?"

"Still fishing, huh?" she said just to be ornery herself. Then she conceded. "I was going to invite you in for coffee, if that's what you had in mind," she said as they turned onto her block.

"I have a better idea. How about you come out to my place?"

Della's heart sank slightly at that. His place meant being with Cully and Ivey and their kids since they all shared the same house. It meant not being alone the way they could be—for a change—at her house.

But maybe he didn't want to be alone with her tonight....

"Sure. Okay," she agreed without much enthusiasm.

But if Yance noticed, he didn't let it show. Rather than heading up the walk to her front porch, he took her elbow and steered her to his truck as they neared it.

"Are you sure Cully and Ivey won't care that we're dropping in this late?" she said as he handed her inside.

"They won't even know we're there," Yance answered with something that looked like mischief in his expression as he closed the door and went around the back of the truck to climb into the driver's side.

They didn't say much beyond pointing out particularly artful pumpkins on the way out to the Culhane ranch. Snow was beginning to fall in tiny flakes, there were no more trick-or-treaters to be seen anywhere and the night had suddenly turned quiet and peaceful.

Unfortunately Della didn't *feel* peaceful. She felt agitated and antsy, and wished this evening had taken a different route than it had.

Yance turned off the main road onto the tree-lined driveway that led onto his property, the same driveway that formed a horseshoe in front of the two buildings that had housed the Culhanes over the years.

The current Culhane house was a two-story clapboard big enough to fill an entire city block all by itself. It was an impressive place—all of Elk Creek had talked about it when Yance's father had built it beside the older family home that had served five generations of Culhanes before that. The most recent home looked like a Southern plantation with its wide porch wrapping around the lower level and the six huge dormer windows on the upper floor.

But Yance didn't pull up in front of that house. Instead, he drove past it to the original home beside it.

Much less impressive, the old house was a plain square saltbox with one end a towering two story and the other a long stretch of single story that shot out from the side like the toe of a boot.

An oversize front door was positioned in the center

of the house with a small porch jutting from it like a stuck-out tongue.

The old house was large—although not as large as the newer version, and nowhere near as nice or as well kept up. Paint was chipping and peeling from it, several of the spindles were missing from the porch railing, there were broken gutters and spots in the roof that were bare of shingles.

It did have all new windows though, Della was surprised to discover. Big, paned windows that looked almost out of place amid the rest of the decay that had obviously occurred as a result of having been vacant for many years.

When Yance stopped the engine, he said, "Wait here for just a minute," and hopped out of the truck.

But he didn't go up to the old Culhane house looming dark and deserted alongside the outer curve of the horseshoe driveway. Instead, he jogged to the newer one as Della watched from the rearview mirror and wondered what he was doing.

Something was up with him, and despite not knowing what it was, she suddenly discovered her disappointment, agitation and antsiness dissolved. In their place simple curiosity, with a dash of renewed excitement, washed in.

Yance was only gone for a few minutes, and when Della saw him come out of the other house again he was carrying a wine bottle, two glasses and what appeared to be a quilt tucked under his arm.

Della got out of the truck before he reached it and met him on the driver's side, thinking that this evening might be taking an interesting turn after all.

"When you said you wanted to go to your house, I thought you meant *your house*," she said with a nod in the direction of the newer abode.

"I did mean my house," he answered with a smile, pointing his chin in the direction of the other structure. "I'm remodeling this one so I can move into it and have it for my own. I thought I'd give you the grand tour."

He led the way up the steps to the dilapidated porch, and Della realized as he unlocked the front door that it wasn't the same front door that had always been there. It was similar in style, with beveled glass in a fan light on the upper third, but the lower portion of it was a design of hand-carved flowers and vines.

"Where did you get this door? It's beautiful," she commented as he pushed it open.

"I made it," he said simply enough, reaching inside to turn on a light and then waiting for her to go in ahead of him.

Della marveled at the talent that had gone into that carving, chalking up yet another thing she hadn't known him capable of before.

She stepped into the entryway then, which was really only the beginning of the construction site. Floorboards were bare, walls were sanded down for retexturing and painting, bald lightbulbs hung where once fixtures had been and exposed wires protruded from wall sockets.

"Wow! You weren't kidding about remodeling. And you didn't just mean a fresh coat of paint here and there," she said as she glanced around.

Yance closed the door behind them. "We were debating about whether or not to have the place bulldozed before the Heller sisters came back to town and filled out some of the ranks of our family. I was against levelin' the house, anyway. But once Clint and Cully got hitched up, well, then it just seemed like a good place for me to go. But it's such an old house and it hasn't been lived in for so long that I needed to do major work on it. Rewire it. Replumb it. Rebuild some of it—like upstairs where I added a couple of bathrooms, turned two of the rooms into one so the master bedroom is bigger…'' He paused, then said, "No sense talkin' about it when I can show you. Want to see?''

"Absolutely," Della said, drawn in by the possibilities that seemed alive all around her.

Yance pointed toward the living room to the right to let her know they could start there, and that was where Della went.

As he explained what he had planned in the way of beamed ceilings, polished wood floors and possibly painted paneling, he poured them each a glass of wine and started a fire in the four-foot fireplace that was framed with the same kind of carving that decorated the front door.

From there, with each of them carrying a wineglass, he showed her the rest of the downstairs.

There was a tiny bathroom he intended to triple in size. The kitchen was empty of any cupboards or appliances and had been extended to include what had originally been a mudroom and enclosed sunporch-turned-laundry-room. Yance was going to add a new laundry room to the side of the house, along with enlarging the other rooms there. One would be a den for himself, and another would be a formal dining room.

Upstairs there were five bedrooms even after he'd combined two, and three more bathrooms. The remodel on that level was further along. Faded cabbage-rose wallpaper was in a pile at one end of the main hall, a sharp contrast to the clean white walls that had already been painted up there, and light fixtures that dated back to the fifties were discarded at the other end, replaced in each room by more-contemporary counterparts that made the place look new.

Della could envision the finished product as Yance talked about what he was still going to do. She had no doubt it would end up rivaling the newer Culhane house in grandeur if not in size. And even in size it was still at least double that of her own house in town.

"Wow," she repeated as they finished looking around and headed back downstairs. "This is quite a project."

Yance shrugged. "I needed something to keep me busy this winter. And now that Cully has a wife and will have more kids before long, it just seemed like a good idea to give the other place over to them."

He set his wineglass on the mantel beside the open bottle and spread the quilt he'd brought from next door on the floor in front of the fire. The temperature in that room had risen enough from the flames to finally allow them to take off their coats, and while she did, Della also slipped off her shoes.

"These are new and they're killing me after all the walking we've done tonight," she said. "Do you mind?"

Yance laughed. "Not if you don't mind if I do the same thing," he said, prying off his cowboy boots.

They both settled on the quilt, Della sitting with her legs under her and to one side, resting her wineglass on her thigh. Yance's legs were bent at the knees, and he braced his forearms on top of them, his own wineglass dangling from one hand.

"This is nice," she said with a sigh of contentment.

"The house or sitting here?"

"The house will be nice when it's finished. But for now I meant it was nice to be sitting here."

"You sound so relieved."

She smiled, slightly embarrassed to admit what she'd been thinking before they'd arrived. But she did it anyway. "When you said you wanted to come out here tonight, I thought we'd be with Cully, Ivey and the kids."

"Instead of alone," he finished for her.

Della nodded with only a scant raising of her chin.

He grinned at her. "Would you rather go next door and visit with them?"

"No, I wouldn't," she admitted.

He just grinned even bigger and leaned back on one elbow, straightening out his long legs toward the fire.

"Could be dangerous, you know, bein' here with me without a chaperon," he said in mock warning.

"I've noticed that you're pretty evil," she agreed facetiously.

"And you're willin' to tempt fate?"

Tonight what she *wasn't* willing to do was share him...

"I think I can take care of myself. If you step out of line, I'll just have to get tough."

"What would it take for me to step out of line?" he asked as if he were considering doing just that.

"Spitting in the fire?" she joked.

He laughed. "Then maybe we're safer than I thought." He took a sip of his wine and watched the flames for a moment.

While he did, Della watched him, studying his profile and marveling all over again at how awesomely attractive he was.

Then, without looking at her, he said, "So, have you been thinkin' about what you were supposed to be thinkin' about from last night?"

She knew what he meant but she wasn't giving any full-blown admissions, so instead she said, "Mmm, maybe."

He glanced up at her from beneath a frown. "Don't be toyin' with me now, Delaware."

She leaned over so she could whisper, "Isn't that the woman's line to the man?"

"I'm not teasin' you."

Oh, he was teasing her, all right, whether he knew it or not. Because there he was, lying next to her, firelight gilding his ruggedly handsome features, his big body loose and inviting and those blue eyes exuding more heat than the flames. He was pure temptation right there within easy reach, and she was itching to touch him, to explore all that glory, to have his arms around her, to have him kissing her, to have him touching her....

"I've been thinking that you were wrong," she told him after a moment, relenting to answer his question as to whether she'd done the thinking he'd assigned her the night before.

"What was I wrong about?"

"I wouldn't have had regrets afterward."

He smiled a slow, pleased smile. "Is that so?"

She answered that with only a raising of her eyebrow.

"I'm not just foolin' around here, though, Del. Know that," he said, and this time his warning was for real.

"I never thought you were."

"I'm serious about you."

Hearing that made her heart take a leap and shook her up a little, too.

But then it occurred to her that she wasn't any less serious about him or she wouldn't be where she was, thinking the thoughts she was thinking, wanting what she was wanting.

"I'm not fooling around here, either," she said very, very quietly, realizing in that moment just how true it was.

He smiled again, kindly, compassionately. But still with a sexy sparkle to his eyes.

Then he sat up and took her wineglass from her hand, placing both hers and his on the floor beyond the quilt. He stretched out once more, braced again on his elbow, and reached for her with only one hand, clasping it behind her neck to pull her down to a kiss that was chaste and yet sweet with promise.

Della kissed him in return, letting her lips part just as his were parted, meeting his tongue when it came to play, playing along, maybe even playing a little more aggressively as something inside her urged her on.

Before she knew it, she was lying on her side, too, facing Yance, kissing still. Only the kisses were deeper suddenly, as he eased her to lie flat and moved close enough to cover her side with the solid length of his body.

Della put her arms around him, flattening her palms firmly to the hard, rolling muscles of his back, wishing his shirt would disappear so she could feel his skin. Wishing it so much she couldn't resist doing something about it.

But it seemed too bold to tear it off him the way she wanted to, so instead she let her hands roll down his back slightly and then rise up with enough pressure to take his shirt with her. Then down and up again, bringing more shirt. And down and up yet again until she'd finessed the tails free of his jeans.

That was when she slipped her hands underneath, to the warm satin of his tautly drawn flesh.

It felt so good. As good as she imagined it looked— hard and sleek, the small of his back widening to an expanse she couldn't span where mountainous muscles rippled beneath her fingertips.

Their kisses were wide-open by then, and tongues did more than play. They danced with intent, a dance that chased and caught and chased again.

Della's thoughts rushed ahead, and she regretted what she'd worn, regretted that she hadn't dressed in a blouse that would come loose from her waistband as easily as Yance's shirt had so that he could put his hands underneath it, too. Because that was what was next on her wish list—to feel Yance's hands against her bare skin as soon as possible.

But there she was in that one-piece jumpsuit zipped to her chin.

If only he'd pull the zipper down!

But Yance's hand was along her jawline, cupping her face, caressing it with slow strokes that paid no attention to the other places she wanted it. To the fact that she wanted to feel his hands on her naked skin so much that just thinking about it arched her spine, bringing her up off the quilt slightly and nearer to him.

Yance still didn't lower that zipper. But he did slide his arms around her, pulling her closer against him and rolling them both to their sides as he kneaded her back with those big, strong hands, the way she longed for him to knead her front.

The trouble was, that was all he did. He held her. He kissed her. He massaged her back. It was as if he were savoring every moment, which was nice, but he wouldn't be hurried through it, wouldn't let *her* hurry through it the way that mysterious something inside her was still urging her to.

And so Della relented to his pace, too, because what else could she do?

She gave in to kisses that really were so incredible she should never have been taking them for granted. She gave in to the soft pleasure of merely being held by him. To the sensual feel of his body pressed to hers. She gave in to the slow arousal of his hands on her back, on her sides, on her waist—even if it was on the outside of the hated jumpsuit.

And little by little, as tiny sparks of delight began to

glitter where before there had been just a sense of urgency, she also gave in to feeling safe, secure, cherished by this man. And she began to relax in a way she hadn't before. To realize that some of that urgency that had been driving her was tension rather than desire. Tension that Yance was finessing out of her much more subtly than she'd finessed his shirt out of his waistband—subtly, slowly, carefully, successfully...

And when she was completely at ease, when there wasn't a trace of stress left in her, when she was blissfully pliable there within the circle of his arms, only then did Yance reach for the jumpsuit's zipper.

He stopped kissing her then, too. Kissing her mouth, at any rate. Instead, he trailed tantalizing kisses down her chin to the sensitive underside of her jawline, to her neck where the high collar began, following the parting zipper inch by inch with kisses that sent sparks all through her bloodstream.

He took the zipper as far as it would go—to her belly button—but he didn't follow it that far with those lovely little kisses. The kisses stopped at the hollow of her throat, then he rose up to recapture her mouth with a new hunger as his hand eased between the open ends the zipper had left and rested on her rib cage.

She hadn't worn a bra, and at that moment that seemed like the only thing she'd done right when she'd dressed today. There was nothing to impede that wondrously strong hand from drawing upward, from closing over her breast, from nestling her kerneled nipple in that perfect palm.

It felt so incredibly good that a moan escaped all on its own as she arched even farther toward him, taking up where they'd left off the night before with a sudden awakening of desire that was more pure than anything that had come before, that was so potent it was as if it had gained power by lying dormant for the past twenty-four hours and then been coaxed so patiently back to life.

Della pressed her hands up his chest to his shoulders, smoothing over them to take the shirt with her, but this time not with the kind of frantic drive with which she'd wanted it out of his waistband earlier. Now she did it Yance's way—with leisurely motions that allowed her to feel the warmth of the skin she was revealing, the honed muscles beneath, the smattering of hair on his chest, the sinew and bone of his shoulders, the power contained in his back, the solid bulge of his biceps.

Yance followed suit, easing the jumpsuit off her shoulders, rolling to his back and bringing Della so she lay on top of him as he ran both hands down her arms to her wrists, to her hands, freeing her from the top half of the jumpsuit at last and leaving her bare breasts pressed to his chest.

That was almost as good as having his hands on them. But not quite, and she had no complaint when he rolled again so that she was on the bottom and he was on top once more.

All at once Yance seemed to lose the ability to contain himself. His lips possessed hers more hungrily, more insistently as his hands reclaimed her breasts, teasing, exploring, tormenting with wicked delight that made her feel as if every nerve ending in her body had risen to the surface, as if every secret recess had been enlivened with a desperate need for his attentions.

Then his mouth sought what only his hands had aroused before, enclosing her nipple in wet, wonderful warmth where his tongue flicked the very crest, sending it into a tight knot. Sucking, nipping, tugging with tender teeth, he aroused in Della a new urgency fiercer than what she'd started out with, lacking all tension, driven only by the wild desires he was stirring in her.

The jumpsuit slipped lower and lower of its own accord, and she was glad of that, glad when it got low enough to kick off. But there still remained the black jeans he wore. Jeans that suddenly felt like the roughest sandpaper against her ultrasensitive skin.

She found his waistband in back, hooked her thumbs into it and let them follow the path around to the snap in front. But there she paused, unsure if she might still be in too much of a hurry.

"Do it, Del," he said between kisses of one breast and then the other.

And she did.

She popped the snap. She unzipped his zipper. She pushed the jeans down as far as she could reach without losing the wonders of his hands, his mouth, finding that she wasn't the only one of them to have left some underwear at home tonight.

He uttered a harsh groan and suddenly rolled away from her to yank his jeans the rest of the way off as if he, too, couldn't endure anything separating them anymore.

And in that moment of distance Della got another thing on her wish list—she got to see him. Stark naked in the firelight and as magnificent as anything her eyes had ever been treated to.

No clothes—no matter how good he looked in them—did justice to that body. That lean, rock-hard specimen of perfect masculine beauty that was a work of art in human form.

And he wanted her. There was no denying the long, thick proof of it there for her to see.

Yance returned to her, his hands and his mouth more masterful now as he kissed her lips, kissed a path back to her breasts. He rid her of the bikini panties she still wore so that this time when they came together it was truly without anything between them. Nothing but that steely shaft of his desire that Della's body was nearly screaming for with a need so great she wasn't sure how much longer she could wait.

She arched more firmly into him, let her own hands course over his back, down to his derriere. And from there they seemed to have a mind of their own as they slid around to his hips, farther around still until she reached him, until she closed one hand around him.

Yance's mouth drew away from the magic he was working at her breast. His head snapped back as her touch seemed to ignite in him what was already burning bright and hot in her.

He rose above her, eased her thighs apart with his knees and then there he was, looming over her, poised and ready for just what she needed, wanted of him.

Slowly at first, he found his home and entered, easing his weight onto her with infinite care, coming ever farther inside until he was finally resting against the very opening of her womb. It felt so extraordinary it took her breath away.

For a brief moment that was how he stayed—very,

very still, not moving, as if letting her become accustomed to having their bodies melded to form one.

And then he began to move. Again, slowly, much the way he'd soothed the tension out of her earlier, as if each drawing out, each slide back inside, was the initial turn of a wheel. Turns that gained a little speed. Then a little more. And more, until they were both moving together with desire unleashed, racing in a mindless passion that vanquished all control, all inhibitions, that drove them beyond thought, beyond anything but the sensations that grew more intense, more overwhelming with each thrust.

Della clung to Yance, unable to keep up with him, giving herself over to him totally. Trusting him to carry her with him on that mad dash.

And carry her with him he did. Catapulting her into a climax so earthshaking, so pure, so exquisite, it was a white-hot explosion that drew her shoulders up off the quilt, that made her dig her fingers into his back, that forced sounds from her throat that she'd never made before.

Deeply, deeply he drove into her, hovering for a split second before he, too, erupted within her in a burst of potent pleasure that made him cry out her name as every muscle in that glorious body tensed.

And for one brief moment it was as if more than their bodies were joined. As if their spirits had fused. As if their hearts had…

And then it ebbed like the tide rushing back out to sea, leaving in its wake a heavy, satiated languor.

Yance relaxed atop her again, kissing her shoulder,

the side of her neck, her ear, pressing his forehead to hers.

"Are you okay?" he asked in a ragged, raspy voice.

"Better than okay. Much, much better," she whispered back because a whisper was all she had the strength for. "Are you okay?" she asked in return, laughing slightly at the thought that he wouldn't be when he felt so indescribably wonderful to her.

He grinned down at her. "I'd say I'm better than okay, too. Much, much better."

He kissed her again, a kiss unlike any that had come before, filled with a new intimacy, a new connection.

Then he slipped out of her and rolled once more to his back, bringing her to lie beside him, to use his chest as her pillow.

When he had her there, he reached for the edge of the quilt and brought it over them both, wrapping them in soft warmth that made it impossible for Della to fight the heavy drowsiness that was descending on her.

But just before she fell all the way asleep, it occurred to her that for the first time in her life she'd just made love to a man other than Bucky.

And nothing about it had seemed anything but right. Very, very right.

Chapter Nine

About three in the morning the fire died, leaving the house cold enough to wake Yance and Della. Yance built a new fire, crawled back under the quilt and they made love a second time, which was more incredible than the first had been. Then they fell into satiated sleep once more.

So when Yance woke again at dawn, the fire was still warming the room and Della was still warming his side, snuggled against him as if that was where she belonged.

He didn't move an inch because the last thing he wanted was to disturb her or the way they were lying. It was just too comfortable, even if they were on the floor, and he liked having her in his arms too much to do anything that would risk losing it.

No, he wanted to savor the feel of her soft, naked

body pressed to him; her leg slung over his; the feel of her silken skin; her hair brushing his shoulder; each breath she exhaled.

And he suddenly had an overwhelming sense that this was the way things were meant to be. That he and Della were meant to be together. In this house. With her kids and any kids he and Della would add to her kids.

He didn't know when his feelings for her had grown so strong. But there they were just the same. He was crazy about her.

He had a clear vision of how the house would look when he was finished with it. And now, into that image came Della. Della in the kitchen, laughing as she set dinner on a table surrounded by Yance and a passel of kids. Della cozied up in the living room in front of this very fireplace, watching old John Wayne movies with him. Della coming into his den on a lazy Sunday afternoon to curl onto his lap, wrap her arms round his neck and liven up an hour or two. Della in the master bedroom upstairs...

Yance closed his eyes and indulged in the mental pictures, wishing the house was completely finished. Wishing Della and the kids were living there already...

But what would she think about it all? he asked himself.

His eyes opened as that question and a lot more shot through his brain to replace the fantasy that had been entertaining him. Questions like, was he competing with a ghost to start up with Della only a year after Bucky's death? What if he was only a proxy? Could

Della see him for the man he was himself? Love him for that alone?

It occurred to him that the answers to a few of those questions were right there in front of his face.

Or, at least, lying by his side.

After all, it hadn't been Bucky's name Della had called out in the throes of passion that second time. She'd known whom she was with, who was making love to her. Her late husband hadn't been on her mind then; Yance was sure of it.

Was Bucky still alive in Della's heart, though?

Probably. To some degree. Because Nancy was still alive in his heart to some degree. But clearly that didn't mean there wasn't room for other people, for *loving* other people, or he wouldn't feel the way he did about Della. About her kids.

And thoughts about those they'd lost also didn't interfere with what he and Della had together, he decided. What they *could* have together. The specters of those late loved ones might have been hanging around for Yance, for Della, for the kids, but that hadn't kept them from enjoying each other and their time together. It hadn't kept Yance and Della from getting closer and closer. From starting up whatever this was they'd started up.

As for poaching on Bucky's territory, Yance reasoned that Della and the kids could only be Bucky's territory if Bucky were still alive. But what about the possibility that he would be competing with cherished memories of his old friend? Wouldn't there always be some other man's standards to live up to? Comparisons being made?

Again, probably.

But was that so daunting? In all the years he and Bucky had been friends, they'd been an even match in most everything. And Bucky had been a good, honorable, decent man. Those were things Yance tried to be himself one way or another.

So could he live with stepping into another man's boots?

He thought he could. If it meant having Della. Having her family as his own...

But something else gave him pause all of a sudden, as another thought popped into his mind.

He recalled Ashley's questions to him during her birthday dinner about whether or not he was pretending that they were the family he'd lost.

It had niggled at him off and on since then, making him wonder if there was any of that in the appeal the Dennehys had for him. And now he had to ask himself more seriously—was he substituting his old friend's ready-made family for Nancy and Jeremy? Was he himself just plugging in replacement parts?

Yance thought about that long and hard. Longer and harder than he'd thought about all the other questions put together. He wanted to be sure that wasn't what he was doing just because he'd reached a time in his life when it had become tougher to be flying solo, tougher and more lonely as he'd watched his brothers both pair up.

It wouldn't be fair to Della or her kids if there was any element of that at all in his feelings for them. And it sure as hell wouldn't be a good way to venture into any kind of commitment.

So he analyzed himself and his motivations. He examined his own feelings, the thoughts he'd been having since he'd taken this new notice of Della, all the while asking himself if he had only fallen in with her and her kids out of a need to fill a gap.

But the more he considered that, the more he knew it wasn't true.

In spite of life having been tougher and lonelier for him since his brothers had married the Heller sisters, it still wasn't the toughest, loneliest time he'd ever spent. The toughest, loneliest time had been after losing Nancy and Jeremy. Yet he hadn't rushed out to fill that gap then.

And if simply filling the gap was what he was doing, he could have done that before now. There had been other women he had gotten close to since Nancy and Jeremy died. Other women who had kids. Yet he'd never even considered taking any of those relationships further than casual dating.

But then, he'd also never felt about them the way he felt about Della and her four kids now.

So, no, Della and those four kids were not just convenient replacement parts.

It was Della herself that he wanted.

Maybe that crush he'd had on her in the eighth grade had been a preview of things to come, because as he lay there with her in his arms, he suddenly knew without a doubt that what he felt for her was as fresh and pure as that had been. No ulterior motives tainted it. It didn't come from loneliness or any other kind of need. It only came from Della and his feelings for her. From how much he enjoyed her, from how much he wanted her.

The truth was that he just plain loved her, and that was all there was to it.

Which led him right back to where he'd started— what would Della think about taking what was between them all the way?

And most important, what did Della feel about him?

Neither of those two questions could be answered by any amount of pondering, by any amount of analyzing.

The answers to them were only in Della's heart.

And the single way for him to get to them was to talk to her about all this.

Which was exactly what he was going to do.

But the one thing Yance knew as he tightened his hold on her was that if what was in her heart wasn't what he hoped it would be, it was likely to break his heart.

Della was all alone in a desert. And yet she was still cold. Cold and alone. And sad. So sad she ached inside.

She recognized the feeling even if she didn't recognize the place, and so she knew what had happened even without really knowing. She'd lost him.

Not Bucky. She knew it wasn't Bucky. She knew she'd lost Bucky long ago.

No, this was a new loss. Another loss.

But who?

A man. She knew it was a man. Someone she cared deeply about. She could tell by the way she felt. Desolate. Scared. So, so alone.

What would she do without him? How could she go on?

Oh, yes, these were the same feelings, all right.

And she couldn't have them again. She couldn't go through this again. She had to get away. She had to get away from the desert. She had to get away from these feelings.

But how could she do any of that?

Then suddenly she wasn't in the desert. She was in her house. And there was crying all around her. Her kids were crying just the way they had when she'd told them Bucky had died. Sobbing. Sobbing.

She was sobbing, too.

I can't do this again...I can't go through this again.... It hurts too bad....

There was a coffin on the stairs. What was it doing on the stairs? And who was in it? Whom had she lost this time?

She crept up the stairs between the casket and the railing, keeping as much distance as she could, carefully, as if something might jump out at her. Not wanting to know who was in it. Needing to know. Afraid of knowing.

But something drove her on. Something told her that the coffin wouldn't disappear until she looked inside. Until she knew who was in it.

The lid was raised, and when she finally reached that part of the casket she forced herself to peer at the body lying there.

Yance. It was Yance.

She'd known it all along.

Now Yance was dead, too.

Her stomach knotted. Everything inside her tight-ened up and turned topsy-turvy. She thought she might be sick.

I can't go through this again...I can't go through this again...I can't go through this again....

Della woke with a start. For a moment she didn't know where she was, why she was wrapped in a blan-ket on the floor of an unfamiliar place. Alone.

And what about Yance? she thought in a panic. The dream was still with her, making her wonder if there had been some truth to it, if something had happened to him and if that was why she was where she was.

She struggled to grasp what was real and what wasn't, finally remembering.

No. Yance wasn't dead. He had been there all night, she remembered. Holding her. Making love to her. He just wasn't there right now.

And with that knowledge came a flood of memory to help fill in the pieces. She was in the house Yance was remodeling, wrapped in the blanket that had cush-ioned those two rounds of lovemaking and kept them warm as they'd slept in each other's arms.

But even knowing where she was, knowing Yance was all right, didn't help the way Della felt.

All the feelings in the dream were alive in her as powerfully as if they had some basis. Feelings she'd had when Bucky had died.

And suddenly she had an intense need to go home. To be on familiar territory. To hug her kids. To lock her door. To get back to normal. To where she didn't have dreams like that. To where she'd stopped suffering the emotions that were going through her at that moment.

There were no sounds of Yance in the house, and with a furtive glance around to make sure he wasn't standing somewhere silently watching her, she lunged out of the quilt, did a fast search for her clothes and got into them in record time, putting on even her shoes and coat.

When Yance came in from the rear of the house carrying an armload of firewood, she knew she must look as if she were ready to make a run for it. But that didn't matter to her. The only thing that mattered was that she get home. That she get to where she wasn't so vulnerable.

"Hi," she said nervously.

"'Mornin'," he answered, looking and sounding confused.

He had on the black jeans from the previous night, but no shirt or shoes or socks. And even though several pieces of chopped wood covered his middle, his strong shoulders and bulging biceps were visible to taunt her with memories of what it had been like to touch them, to lie against them. Flickering memories that brought with them flickering desires...

Della swallowed with some difficulty and forced her gaze upward to his face.

That didn't help much because he looked all too terrific even with the shadow of morning beard shading his strong jawline and his hair sexily tousled from sleep.

But still she fought his appeal.

"I have to go home," she said as if he'd asked for

an explanation. "Kansas could be bringing the kids back from the sleepover anytime."

"It's only 6:00 a.m. She wouldn't be bringin' 'em back this early, would she?"

"It's possible. Anything is possible."

"Are you okay, Del?" Yance asked with a deep frown pulling his brows to nearly meet over those blazing blue eyes that were boring into her at that moment.

She had a flashback of his asking her the same thing after the first time they'd made love. Of the way she'd felt—warm and cherished and satiated.

He had cared if she was okay. Genuinely cared. He cared now. And that was nice. More than nice. It was wonderful to once again have someone think of her, worry about her, want her....

Too wonderful.

"I'm fine," she said in a way that made it clear she wasn't fine at all. So she put what she hoped sounded like a lighter tone into her voice and added, "I just want to get to the house, clean up, change my clothes before the kids get there and can tell I didn't sleep at home last night."

Yance nodded as if he wasn't completely convinced but had to concede that that made some sense. "Guess I won't build up the fire, then. Just let me pull on my boots, and I'll drive you home."

Why did he have to be so attractive? she thought as he set the wood down near the hearth and gave her a view of his broad, muscle-rippled back. Why did the thought of building up that fire, of slipping off his jeans, of making love with him again, have to stir so many things inside her? Why couldn't she just look at him the way she had all those years before? As an acquaintance, as just another cowboy around town? As someone who could disappear at any moment and not make a dent in her life?

But the truth was, as she stood there watching him, feeling the way she did about him, she didn't know how she had ever looked at him as just an acquaintance, as just another cowboy around town. He was so incredibly handsome, so sweet, so nice, so compassionate, so sexy, how could she not have noticed it, appreciated it, been attracted to him? How could she fight it now?

But she needed to. Right at that moment she needed to more than she needed to do anything she could think of.

"Maybe I'll just wait in the truck," she said as her eyes glued themselves to his rear end when he bent over to retrieve his shirt from the floor.

"I'll only be a second," he said, that confusion still evident. "I was hopin' we could have a little talk before I took you home."

"We can talk on the way," she told him pragmatically because she would have agreed to just about anything to get this show on the road, to escape the potent effect he had on her just by being nearby.

Moments later they were in the truck. Yance started the engine, and Della kept herself smashed against the passenger's door, staring straight ahead to avoid all the things that stirred inside her just by looking at him.

But that didn't stop him from looking at her. From watching her. She could feel his gaze on her as if it gave off the heat of a summer sun.

"What did you want to talk about?" she asked, hoping to distract him from staring at her, thinking that nothing he had to say could be as unnerving as that.

He didn't answer immediately, as if he wasn't sure he *did* want to talk to her anymore.

But after he'd put the truck in gear and headed down the driveway away from both Culhane houses, he seemed to give in. "I wanted to talk about how good we are together."

Better than good, was what popped into Della's mind. But with it also came a fresh surge of that same kind of panic she'd had in the dream.

"I have some pretty strong feelin's for you, Della," he said cautiously.

She had some strong feelings for him, too. That was the problem. Strong feelings now. Sharp, unbearable pain later...

"When I woke up this mornin' with you there by my side, in the house, it felt like such a perfect fit that it started me thinking'."

"Too much thinkin' that early can't be healthy," she said, trying to make a joke—albeit a feeble one—to diffuse both the tension that had her tied in knots and whatever he was about to say.

But Yance didn't let her distract him from his goal. "That's a big house," he said. "Big enough for a family. For a man and a woman. For four kids and then some."

"You aren't proposing to me, are you?" she blurted out, sounding as afraid of that as she felt. Her heart was beating so fast and furiously it pounded in her ears, and the need to escape was strong enough to make her wonder how badly she'd be hurt if she threw herself out of the truck at that moment.

Yance glanced over at her, a dark frown marring his handsome features. "Are you sure you're all right?"

"Fine. I'm fine. I just need to get home." Home base where she could cry *Olly olly oxen free* and be safe...

His expression was dubious but he forged on anyway, although his tone became slightly more conversational, almost as if he were teasing her and not actually committing to anything.

"Think you could ever see me as a husband?" he asked without answering her question about this being a proposal.

"You'd make a good husband," she answered ambiguously.

"For you?" he persisted but still with that note in his voice that made it sound casual.

"For anyone. You're a good man," she responded, once more in ambiguous terms, purposely keeping this as impersonal as she could. If that was possible.

"What about you? Can you see yourself as a wife again?"

As *his* wife. Sleeping every night in those arms...

But that wasn't what she said.

"I don't know. I haven't thought about it."

"Would you?"

"Would I what?"

"Would you think about it?"

"I can't," she blurted out again, in a fresh wave of that panic.

"You can't?"

Della's thoughts and feelings were in a muddle. She was more confused than she'd ever been in her life, more torn between wanting Yance, wanting to be with him, maybe even wanting to be his wife, and absolute terror of going through what she'd gone through when she'd lost Bucky, what she'd go through if she ever again lost someone she loved that much. Someone like Yance.

She fought to find a way to explain to him what was going on inside her, fought to keep from blurting out anything else that might offend him. Or hurt him.

Finally she remembered what April had said when she'd crawled into bed with her and she opted for re-counting that to Yance.

"I didn't realize it until this morning, but April isn't the only one of us harboring fears of loving and losing another man in our life," she said when she finished.

She expected him to tell her she was being silly. But he didn't say anything at all. In fact, he appeared to be giving what she'd said a lot of thought as he headed into town.

Then he said, "I felt like that after losin' Nancy and Jeremy. I thought I didn't want any more kids, especially, because buryin' Jeremy was the hardest thing I've ever done."

"So you understand," Della said in relief.

"I understand. I also understand that I got over feelin' that way."

He turned onto her street, quiet at that early hour, and Della counted rolled-up issues of morning news-papers that were waiting on snow-covered doorsteps all up and down the block—hers included when he pulled to a stop at the curb.

He turned off the engine and angled in her direction, stretching a long arm across the seat back but not touching her.

"You can stay shut off from things and people and feelin's, Della. But that's no way to live."

She wasn't shut off from things and people and feelings. She had her kids. She had a full, busy life taking care of them, meeting their needs. She loved them. They loved her.

It was only the thought of allowing Yance into the picture that scared the daylights out of her.

He was just too much of everything that was wonderful, everything Bucky had been. And it was too easy to become accustomed to it all. To depend on it all. To need it all.

It was too easy to lose it all.

And then too devastating.

Better not to get into it in the first place. Better not to indulge, not to become accustomed to what he had to offer. Better not to depend on it, on him. To need him. Then there was no loss. No devastation. No pain...

"What if I tell you I love you, Della?" he said then, serious again.

It made her flinch. She didn't want to hear it. It was too tempting. It touched her too much. It brought to the surface too many of her own feelings for him.

"What if I told you I'd like you to do more than just think about bein' my wife? What if I told you I *want* you to be my wife? That I want your kids to be my kids, too. That I want to add a couple more of our own—''

''No!'' she blurted out yet again as if he were torturing her with his words. ''Don't tell me any of that. Please.''

''Why not?''

''I told you. I can't go through it again, Yance. I can't.''

''Nothin's gonna happen to me, Della. Would you feel better if I went to the doctor and got a clean bill of health so you'd know that?''

''Heart attacks like Bucky had aren't the only thing that take people away. Or strokes like the one Nancy had. You lost Jeremy in the accident that was a result of Nancy's stroke. Accidents happen all the time. And people leave. Mary Alice's father and her mother's boyfriend just left on their own two feet. Things happen....''

''Yeah, they do. Bad things happen. We're both witnesses to that. But good things happen, too. Like our findin' each other after all these years. Like my lovin' you. Like babies bein' born and love bein' made, and life goin' on. If you let it, Del.''

''I can't,'' she repeated, feeling her eyes well up with tears for no reason she could pinpoint. ''I can't.''

''I want you, Delaware. I love you,'' he said so, so softly.

There he was, as appealing as ever a man had been, with his mink-colored hair all ruffled up and barely finger combed, his chiseled jaw whiskered and those earth-shatteringly blue eyes searching her face.

She was already in deeper than she wanted to be,

she realized, because she was hurting now at the thought that she was going to walk into her house and leave him behind, only to see him in passing from here on, just the way she had all those years before.

But as bad as she was hurting now, it was nothing compared to what she knew it could be—*would* be— if she let this get any further. If she admitted that she loved him, too. If she actually did marry him, and then lost him.

"No. No. I just…I can't," she said in a rush. "I'm sorry. I guess I should never have gotten involved in this…with you… I guess I wasn't ready after all."

He opened his mouth to say more, but before he could, she flung the truck door wide, jumped out and nearly ran for her house.

For her house and the safety she was sure she'd find inside.

Chapter Ten

Della had showered but she was still in her bathrobe when Kansas brought the kids home later that morning. All four of them talked at once, telling their mother what they'd done since she'd dropped them off. Della barely heard any of it as, one by one, she gave each of them a long hug.

Then they bounded off to watch cartoons, and she offered her sister a cup of coffee.

"I have news, or maybe you already know," Kansas said as Della poured two mugs of the freshly brewed stuff and brought them to the table where Kansas waited.

"I haven't heard anything newsworthy," Della informed her as she sat across from her sister.

"Then you don't know that Savannah had her baby last night about ten?"

Mixed emotions ran through Della at that. She pushed aside the envious ones and focused on the ones that were happy for her best friend. "She did? What did she have?"

"A boy. A big one—eight pounds, ten ounces."

"And are they both okay?"

"Perfect in every way. Clint said Savannah wanted you and Ivey to be the first to know, but he'd called over here and you weren't home. He thought you might be at my place. I told him I'd track you down but only if he told me why—that was how I found out." Kansas gave Della a sly glance. "I tried calling and calling you—until midnight last night and again first thing this morning. But there was no answer."

Della ignored the quizzical edge to her sister's tone and said, "I'll bet Savannah and Clint are both on cloud nine."

"They're ecstatic. But where were you?" Kansas asked outright then, her curiosity obviously getting the better of her.

Della debated through several sips of coffee how much to tell Kansas. But in the end she made a full confession, confiding even her dream and what had happened this morning.

"So, let me get this straight," Kansas said when Della had finished. "You love Yance so you rejected him and don't intend to see him again except in passing because you're too afraid of losing him?"

"Don't make it sound ridiculous. It isn't. You love Linc—think about what it would be like if the phone rang right this minute and someone told you he was dead. Gone forever in the blink of an eye. How would you feel?''

''Indescribably desolate. Horrible. Probably worse than I can even imagine.''

''And how many times would you want to go through it?''

''Is Yance dying?''

''No, of course not. But anything can happen. And men don't only leave by dying these days. They just leave, too.''

''So you don't want to take the risk.''

''No, I don't.''

''And how do you feel now that you've gotten rid of that risk—and Yance along with it?''

Della frowned into her coffee cup. ''I feel relieved.'' She hesitated. ''And bad, too,'' she admitted to both herself and her sister.

''And I'll bet you feel more of the bad feelings than of the relief.''

''For the moment. But it'll pass.''

''Feeling bad would also pass if you got together with Yance and something happened. But in the meantime you could have a lot of good feelings that you're denying yourself now.''

Della just shook her head, thinking that Kansas didn't understand.

''Life is full of losses, Del,'' Kansas said. ''Someday we'll lose Mom and Dad. Your kids and my Danny will grow up and leave home, maybe leave Elk Creek or even the state of Wyoming—that's a kind of losing. Even if you married Yance and lived happily together for the next sixty years, eventually one of you will face losing the other just the way Linc or I will face it, the way half of most every couple will. You just can't be alive and not have loss.''

"I've already had my share," Della insisted.

"Does that mean that you would rather have been an orphan than go through what you'll go through when Mom and Dad die? That you'd rather not have your kids because one day they'll leave home? Does it mean that you would rather have never met Bucky at all, or fallen in love with him, or married him and had the time you had together so you would never have had to suffer losing him?''

"No, of course not," Della said.

"But you would give up a man you love now rather than risk that someday—maybe not for a long, long time, but someday—you could lose him?''

"There you go making it sound ridiculous again. But don't you see? Mom and Dad, the kids, they're all here already. I can't avoid facing whatever I'll have to with them. But letting things go even further with Yance, that's just asking for more heartache.''

"Not if you're together until you're both 107 and then you die together in a tornado.''

Della rolled her eyes at her sister's exaggerations.

"Okay, now I am being ridiculous. But you're not even thinking about the possibility that the two of you could have a long life together. That you could have Yance and a gazillion full, happy years with him be-fore—and *if*—you ever had to deal with anything like what you've just gone through over Bucky. You're cut-ting short any chance for love and happiness...for *life,*

Della, because something *might* happen. How much sense does that make?''

''A lot when you feel the way I felt when Bucky died. The way I felt in that dream and when I woke up from it this morning.''

''I know it's been hard for you—''

''And for the kids.''

''And for the kids. But look at it this way—maybe whatever force brought you and Yance together now is offering Yance as a consolation for all you guys have been through. He's an opportunity for you to be happy again. For the kids to have a father. I can't stand for you to turn your back on that.''

Della shook her head, wishing she could see all this in as positive a light as Kansas did. But how could she do that when those feelings that had been reawakened by the dream were lingering to remind her just how negative an end could be waiting if she didn't protect herself now, while she still could.

''Come on, Del,'' Kansas cajoled. ''Last night was the beginning of a new life for Savannah and Clint's baby. Let today be the beginning of a new life for you, too. For you and the kids. Stop giving in to your fears and follow your heart.''

She *was* following her heart. The part of it that hurt all over again.

But even as that part of her heart had her in its grip, she knew there was another part that longed to do just what Kansas was advocating. That loved Yance and wanted to tell him that. To accept all he had to offer...

Which was why she was so torn yet again.

''Just think about it,'' her sister urged. ''And talk to

the kids. From all the stories I heard about Yance last night it seems to me they're pretty taken with him. Even April, no matter what she told you before.''

"I don't know," Della said in what sounded almost like a lament.

"I know you'd be crazy not to grab that man. He's good for you. He loves you." Kansas stood to go but leaned over close to Della's ear and added, "And you love him. So quit worrying about the bad things that might never come about anyway and enjoy the good things that are happening."

"Easy for you to say," Della joked, or tried to at least.

"Easy for you to do, too, if you'd just let it be."

Kansas patted Della on the shoulder and left, hollering goodbye to the kids as she went down the hallway and out the front door, leaving Della to stare into space with Kansas's words spinning in her head.

Kansas just didn't understand, she thought, shying away from her sister's advice.

Kansas didn't know what it was like to wake up in the middle of the night, reach for Linc on the other side of the bed and then remember with a fresh surge of agony that he was dead. Kansas didn't know what it was like to be so weighted with grief that it sapped every ounce of energy. She didn't know what it was like to feel as if she couldn't make it through another day without Linc. To walk into a room and expect to find him there only to realize he'd never be there again. She didn't know what it was like to ache for the comfort of his arms, his kisses. To bury a tearstained face in one of his old shirts just to smell a smell that was all there was left of him.

Kansas just didn't know how much it hurt. She'd had sadness in her life before meeting Linc, but not sorrow. Not bone-crushing, spirit-suffocating, debilitating sorrow.

Kansas only knew that she was going home now to a flesh-and-blood man who loved her. That when she walked in the door the handsome face she adored would be there to greet her. The voice that was like a soothing balm to her would wash over her. She only knew that if any problems arose, she had Linc there to turn to. That if she felt like gliding straight into his arms they'd be there, open and ready to enfold her in them...

Just the way Yance could be there for me...

Della didn't know where that thought had come from. But there it was. Reminding her that she, too, could once again have all those good things, all those things that would make her happy, that would make her feel secure, that would make her feel loved.

If only she took the risk that came with them...

There must have been a commercial break in the cartoons, because suddenly all four kids came into the kitchen, clamoring for the refrigerator and the pantry.

All except Billy, who was searching for his Halloween sack full of candy.

"Not until after lunch and then you can only have one piece," Della said, distracted from her thoughts. "You know the rules about sweets."

Talk to the kids...

Kansas's words repeated themselves in her mind.

"Come and sit over here a minute, would you all?" Della heard herself say before she even knew she was going to say it. "I want to talk to you."

"Oh-oh. Did we do somethin' bad?" Nic asked.

"No. Nobody did anything bad. I just want to know what you guys think of Yance."

"I like him," Billy announced flat out, his mother's streak of bluntness showing.

"Me, too," Nic chimed in.

"He's nice," April allowed.

"And he's a babe," Ashley gushed.

Unanimous accolades. That was a good sign.

Still, Della trod very carefully in asking her next question. "What would you all think about having him be a part of our family?"

That stalled the quick replies.

"You mean like he'd be our dad?" Nic asked after a moment.

"I don't know. Maybe."

"He's not our dad," Billy declared defensively.

"He'd be our stepdad," Ashley clarified as if her brother were a dunce. Then she altered her focus to Della. "Are you gettin' married to him?"

"Right now I'm only thinking about some things," was all Della could commit to. "But what if I did? How would you guys feel about it?"

"I like him," Nic said, parroting his brother's earlier words.

"We wouldn't forget Dad," Billy said as if it were a challenge.

"Never. Not in a million years. No matter who ever comes into our lives," Della assured.

"Okay, then," Billy conceded. "Yance's fun. And Linc says he's a good man."

That surprised Della. "When did you talk to Linc about Yance?"

"Last night. I was feelin' kinda bad 'cause Dad wasn't there for trick-or-treatin', but I had a good time with Yance anyhow and I told Linc about it."

Della knew her oldest son had a case of hero worship for his uncle and that it was likely that anything Linc said about Yance would carry great weight. "What did Linc say?"

"That Yance was one of the goodest men he ever knowed and that if somethin' ever happened to him and he couldn't never not come back to be with Danny, he can't think of no one who'd be a gooder man to look after him instead. Then he said he knowed my dad well 'nuff to tell me that my dad would be glad for me to have Yance around, too. So, I guess it'd be okay if you married him or somethin'."

"I think it'd be okay, too," Ashley agreed. "I think it'd be romantic," she finished with a dreamy voice.

"He's nice," Nic added, mimicking April this time.

But April still hadn't given a more firm endorsement than that.

"What about you, honey? What do you think?" Della asked her younger daughter directly.

"I like Yance, too," she offered conservatively. "And I think he's nice. But what about if he goes away after later?"

"That scares me, too," Della admitted. "But Linc is right—Yance is a good man. A man I think we can trust not to leave like Mary Alice's father and her mother's boyfriend did. A man we can trust never to hurt us if he can help it.'' And as she assured her daughter of that, Della realized it was true. Yance was a man of his word. A man who had no problem making and keeping commitments.

"But what if he died like Daddy did?" April persisted, touching that raw nerve in her mother.

Della didn't answer immediately. It was as if she'd come to the final fork in the road and she had to make a decision about which way to go. Which part of her own heart to follow.

The part ruled by fear.

Or the part ruled by the feelings she had for Yance.

"That's jus' dumb," Billy piped up before Della had said anything. "That's like Mom sayin' our Halloween candy'll give you cavities. We still eat it anyway, and it didn't give us no cavities yet."

"If April don't want her candy, I'll have it," Nic offered.

"I want my candy!" April insisted.

"Then maybe you'll get a cavity," Billy said pragmatically.

"I'll brush my teeth extragood. But nobody's gettin' my candy but me!"

The bickering took all four of them back into the living room, leaving Della alone with her thoughts once again.

Was she being dumb—the way Billy thought April was—not to enjoy the good now and just hope that the bad never came?

It wasn't easy to override the fear of suffering another loss, if it came to that. But the more Della considered her sister's analogies and her son's, the more she realized she just might be being dumb at that.

A piece of cake could end up adding a pound. A piece of candy could end up producing a cavity. To have children was to accept that one day they would leave the nest.

None of those eventualities was worth denying the pleasures that came first.

Sure, committing herself to Yance could lead to more heartache if something bad happened down the road. But there was always the chance that it might not.

And even if it did, in the meantime she could have the laughter, the fun, the comfort, the companionship, the love she'd found with him. Things she couldn't for the world wish she hadn't had with Bucky for all the years they were married just because it had ended tragically and much too soon.

"April! Would you come in here again, please?" she called to her younger daughter.

"It's not a commercial," April called back.

"Come in here anyway," Della said, thinking that apparently their conversation of moments before hadn't disturbed April too much.

The pigtailed seven-year-old ran in, clearly impatient to have whatever her mother wanted over and done with as quickly as possible.

"You never did tell me if you thought it would be all right to have Yance be a part of our family."

"Do you think he's gonna die like Daddy did?"

"No, I don't think he is. Not for a long, long, long

time, after you're all grown-up. But I can't say that for sure.''

April frowned through consideration of that. Then she shrugged. ''I guess it'd be okay. I like him. I just don't want him to go away after just a little while. Not till I'm *really* old—like twenty or somethin'.''

Della laughed at her daughter's perception of what was really old.

''So you'd be all right with my getting together with Yance?''

''Okay. I guess so. Now can I go watch cartoons? This is my favorite one.''

''Sure,'' Della conceded.

Well, she had everyone's blessing, she realized. Nothing was standing in her way.

Except her own fears.

There had been a lot of those since Bucky's death. Being afraid of how she would handle emergency situations and make decisions without him. Being afraid of how she could ever cope with all the responsibilities of four kids and a house on her own. Even being afraid of that first winter storm a week ago and the possibility of being stranded by it.

But so far, she'd handled an emergency here and there, she'd made any number of decisions, she'd coped with all the responsibilities of four kids and a house just fine. And certainly the snow had brought with it a good turn in Yance.

But now she was faced with yet another fear. A bigger fear than all the others before.

The fear of loving and losing again.

It occurred to her that the difference between the fear

she was in the throes of now and the others she'd had since Bucky's death was that she hadn't had a choice about facing the others. She'd had to. She hadn't had the luxury of letting those other fears control her because, like it or not, afraid or not, she'd had to deal with emergencies that arose and making decisions and the kids and the house.

But this time she had a choice. Whether to give in to the fear or fight it. To act in spite of it. To follow that part of her heart that cried out for Yance and ignore that part that was enmeshed in fear.

She didn't like the idea of being controlled by any fear, she realized. Founded, unfounded, no matter what, she didn't want to be a person who refused anything out of fear.

Let alone a happy life with a man who loved her. A man she loved. A man she wanted to spend her future with.

"So there's your answer," she said out loud.

Worrying about what might happen, about losing Yance, was one thing, but to deny herself a life with him because of it was something else again.

It was as dumb as Billy had said it was.

And she suddenly knew with crystal clarity that she loved Yance. That he loved her. And that those were the things that were truly important. More important than any fear. Than any concern. Than any worry about what could happen in the future.

Della stood then and went to the telephone, picking up the receiver and dialing her sister's number.

Because she wasn't about to be dumb anymore.

And she knew Kansas wouldn't object to turning right around and coming back to baby-sit.

While Della ran a very important errand.

A light snow had begun to fall again by the time Della followed the driveway up to the old and new Culhane houses. She bypassed the newer one and parked in front of the older.

She had no idea if that was where Yance would be. She only hoped that on a snowy Sunday afternoon that's where she'd find him because she didn't want to do what she'd come to do with the audience that would be at the other place.

She turned off the engine and got out of her car, closing the door gingerly. Not because she was skulking in. It was just a result of the trepidation she felt. The tentativeness. The uncertainty of how she'd be received by a man who must surely think she was out of her mind by now and might have reconsidered what he'd proposed to her earlier. He might even have decided that he was better off without the nutso she'd become in the past several hours, and if that was the case he wasn't likely to be too thrilled to see her.

Not that she could blame him.

But she prayed that wasn't the case as she climbed the steps onto the front porch.

Luck was with her—he was inside. She caught sight of him through the big picture window before she knocked on the front door next to it.

He'd shaved and probably showered, too, because his hair was tamer than it had been earlier. Gone were the black jeans of the previous night and this morning, replaced by a pair of blue jeans that were faded, torn here and there and paint splattered.

And that was all he had on.

No socks, no shoes, no shirt.

It seemed strange, but Della was less absorbed in guessing the circumstances that might have led him to be here only partially clothed than she was in simply drinking in the vision he presented.

He stood facing the fireplace, his hands far apart on the mantel, bending over as if to peer into the firebox, his head low between his arms, almost like a runner catching his breath.

It took Della a moment to catch hers as she stood there watching him, letting her gaze slide from big, powerful hands splayed against the carved oak mantel; to wrists that were inexplicably sexy; to taut, thick forearms and biceps swollen with strength; along shoulders so wide they looked as if they could carry the weight of the world; down the wide V of a back that was wrought with the hills and valleys of well-cut muscles; to that to-die-for derriere....

And mixed with her uncertainty and trepidations and worry about his response to her coming here, there was suddenly a rush of desire almost as urgent as she'd felt the night before. Desire to let her hands travel the same path her glance just had, to have him hold her, kiss her, make love to her again.

Please don't let me have ruined this, she said in silent supplication as she took a deep breath, shored up her courage and finally knocked on the door.

At the sound of that he did a push-up off the mantel

and turned, looking out the picture window before he headed for the door.

His eyes met hers in that instant and his initial frown of curiosity changed to a more serious expression, making Della's stomach lurch.

Please don't let me have ruined this...

Yance opened the door then, letting surprise replace his sober frown. "Della?" he said as if he didn't recognize her.

"Hi," she said feebly, giving him a little wave that she regretted because it made her feel foolish.

"Did you forget something?" he asked as he pushed the tattered screen door wide enough to let her in.

"I think I forgot myself," she said slightly under her breath as she stepped into the entryway, fighting the urge to step into his arms instead.

"You forgot yourself?" he repeated, confused.

"I forgot that until the last year I was never such a fraidy-cat—as my kids would call me."

She couldn't help herself. She had to walk into the living room even though he hadn't invited her to. It just seemed more familiar to her, better ground from which to do what she'd come to do.

The quilt they'd shared was still on the floor there, and even without a fire burning in the fireplace the room was still warm. And yet, warm or not, more familiar or not, she couldn't bring herself to just launch into what she wanted—*needed*—to say. Her courage wavered too much for that.

So once she'd made it to the center of the room, she spun on her heels to face Yance, finding him leaning a brawny shoulder against the side of the arch that connected the living room with the foyer, his arms crossed over that chest she wanted so badly to rest her head on.

She swallowed with some difficulty, pointed her chin in his direction and said, "Were you working on something?"

"The furnace. Then I was gonna do some paintin'. But I had the furnace turned on too high, got too hot and was tryin' to cool off before I got started again."

That answered her curiosity about his being only half-dressed. But clearly he still had a lot of curiosity of his own about her.

"Don't get me wrong—I'm glad to see you," he said. "But what are you doin' out here?"

"I came to talk to you," she answered dimly.

He nodded, but that was as much as he was investing. He stayed where he was, kept on staring at her and just waited for her to go on.

Della swallowed again and did her best. "I had a dream this morning that I didn't tell you about," she began, detailing the dream for him and all it had made her feel, letting him know that was what he'd come in on with that armload of firewood earlier.

"The last thing I expected," she continued, "was for you to start talking about how you felt about me and the kids, about us moving in here."

"And you were in the worst frame of mind to hear it," he guessed.

"You scared me to death," she confirmed. "All I could think was that I couldn't go through losing you, too. I know that sounds silly. Kansas told me so. Even Billy—in a roundabout way—let me know it was dumb to reject what we could have together because of the fear of what could happen later on. But at that moment—''

''You were a fraidy-cat,'' Yance said wryly.

''I was terrified.''

''But here you are now.''

''But here I am now.''

''How come?''

She knew she had to take the leap. Right then. It just wasn't easy.

But after gathering a little more courage, she said, ''Because I love you, too, Yance. Because I want to be with you. Here in this house. Because I want what you want and I couldn't let the fear have its way with me.''

A slow smile stretched his supple lips at that, as if he were thinking about having *his* way with her.

But he didn't budge from leaning against the wall.

Instead, in a quiet voice, he said, ''Nothin's gonna happen to me, and I'm not goin' anywhere, Della.''

It was funny how reassuring it was just to hear those words. As if he had the power to ward off anything bad from ever happening. To him. To her. To the kids.

But of course that was only an illusion, and so she said, ''I hope not. I don't think I could live through losing you.''

He shoved away from the wall then and crossed to her, giving her her heart's desire by wrapping his arms around her and pulling her close.

''I love you, Delaware,'' he said into her hair.

''I love you, too,'' she whispered, filling her hands with the smooth, hard silk of his back.

"Will you marry me?"

A simple question said with such sincerity it made tears well up in her eyes. "Yes, I'll marry you."

"And come to live here with me and let me be a dad to your kids and have a couple more to boot?"

"Tall order," she joked to keep from crying even for joy.

"I'm a tall guy."

She laughed and looked up at him. "That's true enough."

"So what do you say?"

"The house is just too great for me to pass up," she teased. "Guess I'll have to agree to anything to get it."

He squeezed her playfully.

"You're gonna get it, all right," he said with a wicked lilt to only one eyebrow.

Then he kissed her, softly, warmly, sweetly at first. A kiss that said *Hello and welcome home.*

But it didn't stay that way for long before passion ignited between them all on its own and ran through them like a flash fire.

Off came her coat, her sweater, her jeans and all her underwear.

Off came the only thing he had on—his jeans—and he scooped her up into his arms to take her the distance to the quilt again.

Their kisses turned openmouthed and hungry. Their hands explored, aroused, teased and tormented. All with a new confidence, a new boldness.

If there had been any inhibitions before, they disappeared now. Della gave herself to Yance totally, holding nothing back, reveling in his every touch, his every kiss, his every caress, savoring the feel of his big, hard-muscled body, learning each glorious inch, claiming it as her own.

And when they both could contain their desires no longer, he found his home inside her, setting off a thunderous explosion of ecstasy that melded their bodies, their spirits, their souls. That united them more completely than any words could, leaving them joined for life as they each eased back from a peak that wiped away all that had ever separated them.

"I love you, Delaware," Yance said in a gravelly, passion-ravaged voice as he rolled them both to their sides so he could hold her tightly against him.

"I love you, too," she answered much the same way.

"Say you'll still be my wife."

"I'll still be your wife."

"And I'll always be here for you."

"And I'll always be here for you."

He chuckled deep in his throat. "No, I'm telling you that. *I'll* always be here for you. Nothing will ever take me away. At least nothing I can ever do anything about."

"I know," she whispered, pressing a tender kiss to his naked chest, just above his heart.

A heart that was strong and true, she thought, blissfully free of any more fears.

Because somewhere inside her own heart she knew that Yance was what Kansas had said he was—a second gift she'd been given. And that second gift wouldn't be taken from her the way the first had been. Forevermore she and Yance would be together. Would be a family. And would have exactly what they had at that moment...

Pure, powerful, potent love.

That would last a lifetime.

A long, long lifetime.

*   *   *   *   *

International bestselling author

JOAN JOHNSTON

**continues her wildly popular Hawk's Way
miniseries with an all-new, longer-length novel**

THE SUBSTITUTE GROOM

HAWK'S WAY

August 1998

Jennifer Wright's hopes and dreams had rested on her summer wedding—until a single moment changed everything. Including the *groom*. Suddenly Jennifer agreed to marry her fiancé's best friend, a darkly handsome Texan she needed—and desperately wanted—almost against her will. But U.S. Air Force Major Colt Whitelaw had sacrificed too much to settle for a marriage of convenience, and that made hiding her passion all the more difficult. And hiding her biggest secret downright impossible…

**"Joan Johnston does contemporary Westerns
to perfection."** —*Publishers Weekly*

Available in August 1998
wherever Silhouette books are sold.

Take 2 bestselling love stories FREE

Plus get a FREE surprise gift!

The World's Most Eligible Bachelors are about to be named! And Silhouette Books brings them to you in an all-new, original series....

World's Most Eligible Bachelors

Twelve of the sexiest, most sought-after men share every intimate detail of their lives in twelve never-before-published novels by the genre's top authors.

Don't miss these unforgettable stories by:

Dixie Browning

MARIE FERRARELLA

Jackie Merritt

Tracy Sinclair

BJ James

RACHEL LEE

Suzanne Carey

Gina Wilkins

VICTORIA PADE

MAGGIE SHAYNE

Anne McAllister

Susan Mallery

Look for one new book each month in the **World's Most Eligible Bachelors** series beginning September 1998 from Silhouette Books.

Silhouette®

Available at your favorite retail outlet.

HERE COME THE
Virgin Brides!

Celebrate the joys of first love with more unforgettable stories from Romance's brightest stars:

SWEET BRIDE OF REVENGE
by Suzanne Carey—June 1998 (SR #1300)

Reader favorite Suzanne Carey weaves a sensuously powerful tale about a man who forces the daughter of his enemy to be his bride of revenge. But what happens when this hard-hearted husband falls head over heels...for his wife?

THE BOUNTY HUNTER'S BRIDE
by Sandra Steffen—July 1998 (SR #1306)

In this provocative page-turner by beloved author Sandra Steffen, a shotgun wedding is only the beginning when an injured bounty hunter and the sweet seductress who'd nursed him to health are discovered in a remote mountain cabin by her gun-toting dad and *four* brothers!

SUDDENLY...MARRIAGE!
by Marie Ferrarella—August 1998 (SR #1312)

RITA Award-winning author Marie Ferrarella weaves a magical story set in sultry New Orleans about two people determined to remain single who exchange vows in a mock ceremony during Mardi Gras, only to learn their bogus marriage is the real thing....

And look for more VIRGIN BRIDES in future months, only in—

▼ *Silhouette* ROMANCE™

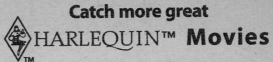 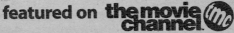

Silhouette

SPECIAL EDITION ®

That's My Baby! ™

Don't miss these heartwarming stories coming to
THAT'S MY BABY!—only from
Silhouette Special Edition®!

June 1998   LITTLE DARLIN'
by Cheryl Reavis (SE# 1177)
When cynical Sergeant Matt Beltran found an abandoned
baby girl that he might have fathered, he turned to compassionate foster mother Corey Madsen. Could the healing
touch of a tender family soothe his soul?

August 1998   THE SURPRISE BABY
by Nikki Benjamin (SE# 1189)
Aloof CEO Maxwell Hamilton married a smitten Jane Elliott
for the sake of convenience, but an impulsive night of
wedded bliss brought them a surprise bundle of joy—and a
new lease on love!

October 1998 FATHER-TO-BE
by Laurie Paige (SE# 1201)
Hunter McLean couldn't exactly recall fathering a glowing
Celia Campbell's unborn baby, but he insisted they marry
anyway. Would the impending arrival of their newborn
inspire this daddy-to-be to open his heart?

THAT'S MY BABY!
Sometimes bringing up baby can bring surprises...
and showers of love.

Available at your favorite retail outlet.